Thinner than blood

The day before she died from a massive haemorrhage, Maud Witherspoon, a spiteful, bed-ridden old lady who had manipulated her family for years, elected to change her will. Instead of leaving half her money to her son and half to her two grandchildren, she tried to bequeath it all to a charity providing help for youngsters living rough.

A seemingly straightforward domestic tragedy quickly turned into a murder hunt as the local CID were alerted to the case by a series of anonymous letters. Was the troublemaker simply guessing at the connection between Maud's death and her money, or did somebody *know* something?

As Maud's granddaughter Deborah goes missing with her pet cat, a fatal attack of bronchial asthma brings the death toll to two in the unhappy Witherspoon household.

Finally, an exhumation reveals proof of the method of Maud's murderer and the police investigation widens dramatically into the search for a frightened schoolgirl and the killer of more than one member of a respected GP's family.

As in her previous novel, *Murderous remedy*, Stella Shepherd's medical background authentically enriches an intricate story of evil, cruelty and greed in a setting both deceptively normal and instantly recognizable.

Also by Stella Shepherd

Black justice (1988)
Murderous remedy (1989)

THINNER
THAN BLOOD

Stella Shepherd

Constable London

First published in Great Britain 1991
by Constable & Company Ltd
3 The Lanchesters, 162 Fulham Palace Road
London W6 9ER
Copyright © 1991 by Stella Shepherd
The right of Stella Shepherd to be
identified as the author of this work
has been asserted by her in accordance
with the Copyright, Designs and Patents Act 1988
ISBN 0 09 470670 0
Photoset and printed in Great Britain by
Redwood Press Limited, Melksham, Wiltshire

A CIP catalogue record for this book
is available from the British Library

For Kathleen

1

People were wrong about hell. It wasn't an inferno which rang with the cries of tormented multitudes; that implied a sense of community spirit, of comrades at one in misfortune. No, thought Maud Witherspoon, hell was solitude and unending boredom. Only powerlessness linked the two concepts . . . or in her case, powerlessness and pain.

She shifted her position in the bed with anticipatory caution, then slumped back exhausted. There were still three hours to go before her visitor arrived, yet she could do nothing to pass the time. The large-print library books were unsuitable, radio didn't appeal, and the one occupation she really craved, tapestry, was impossible. Worse than any of this was the sour recognition that she was actually looking forward to a call from the likes of Gertrude Weddell Grant, vice-president of the Ladies' Friendship Guild, a woman she had always despised. Diversion at any price: no doubt if the milkman were to step inside he could afford a similar measure of entertainment.

With a snort of disgust, Maud began to pull the sheet towards her chin, but checked the movement as a skewer of pain transfixed her thumb. She held her breath while the throbbing subsided, then lifted both her hands and stared at them. It was hard not to be bitter; no one seeing these hands in their current state could believe that they had once been her most admired feature. Pale and shapely, enhanced by diamonds and opals, they had plied fine needles and ivory keyboards with equal grace and competence. Now they were stiff, ugly and almost useless, only one manifestation of a general process of bodily self-destruction.

Rheumatoid arthritis . . . that relentless, debilitating disease had robbed her of both dignity and independence. She was a prisoner in this room, hostage to her daughter-in-law's sullen care and the frigid, dutiful attentions of her son. Once the children had brightened up each day with their chatter, but now Deborah was as withdrawn as her mother and Martin had better things to do with his time.

Resentfully she glared across the room. The powerlessness was hardest of all to bear. She, who had spent a lifetime in command of situations, now had nothing to control. She didn't even reside under her own roof any more, but was an indefinite guest of her doctor son Neville, tolerated only because it might have besmirched his precious reputation to pack her off to a nursing home as he could have done years ago. Money was not an issue; she had plenty.

Furtive sounds in the hall reminded her that Lynn was creeping about the house. Maud pursed her narrow lips. She had never understood how Neville could have married such a passive creature when a girl with brains and character had been his for the taking. Lynn brought out all the stuffed shirt in him, and – dare she think it? – the bully. It was a syndrome well understood by Emily Brontë. What were the words she had given to Heathcliff? 'The more the worms writhe, the more I yearn to crush out their entrails!' Yes, Lynn made people feel like that.

Responding to an association of ideas, Maud reached out her twisted right hand and pressed a nearby button. Neville had rigged up an alarm device for her when she had become bedridden; it rang with a buzzing sound to distinguish it from the doorbell. Maud heard the distant burr in the kitchen and nodded slowly with satisfaction. In five minutes or so Lynn would enter the room wearing an apron with a duster ostentatiously hanging from its pocket, and ask what was wanted. That would be time enough to think of something.

*

8

''Bye, Aileen.' Deborah watched as her friend stood up in the swaying bus and jammed herself into the queue which filled the central aisle.

'Don't forget to ask your dad about the party,' urged Aileen as she waited to alight. 'It *is* tomorrow night.'

'I won't. I'll let you know in the morning.'

'You'd better.' With a gay wave, Aileen vanished in the sea of identical blue uniforms which spilled out on to the pavement at the Clarkwood Estate stop.

Deborah peered through the grimy window and saw the mass disperse into globules of two or three girls, some heading for the baker's shop on the corner, some for the newsagent's, others going straight home to their cramped semi-detached houses. Aileen was now laughing with another girl, Sharon, and looked as if she hadn't a care in the world.

With a lurch the bus set off again, and Deborah clutched the back of the seat in front. She badly wanted to go to this party – there was never any fun at home. Father's decrees had shaped her life as long as she could remember: no television until all homework was done, and even then only news or nature programmes, no teenage magazines with their 'unhealthy preoccupations', no pop records ('mindless thumping'), no make-up ('unnecessary muck on a young girl's face'), no staying out after eleven – and no boys. The party threatened to contravene at least three of these edicts, but Mother had agreed to act as intermediary this time so there was a little bit of hope.

After ten minutes of erratic progress through Nottingham's outer suburbs the bus took a smoother course to the village of Thorbeck. Thorbeck had a picture-postcard centre, with a Norman church, a pub with stocks, and rows of Queen Anne cottages. A stream meandered past the well-tended greensward on its lazy journey to the Trent. The village was surrounded by open country, and high-quality modern housing nestled in discreet culs-de-sac between clusters of farm buildings.

Deborah stepped down alone on to the pavement alongside the greensward, and trotted towards the road leading to her parents' large detached house. Every house in the immediate neighbourhood was owned by professional people. 'Aren't you lucky,' Aileen was always saying – yet surely she was the lucky one.

Deborah entered the house through the kitchen door and heard the distant roar of the vacuum cleaner. Following the noise to its source, she found her mother in the dining-room, cleaning with an air of suppressed anger.

'Hello, Deborah,' said Lynn Witherspoon, clicking off the power so that the machine subsided with a defeated drone. 'Good day at school?'

She looked defeated herself, thought Deborah, now that she was no longer physically active. Her shoulders sagged, a network of lines seemed to drag at her eyes and mouth, and her brown hair was quite grey at the front. How old was Mother? Forty-one, nine years younger than Father. That *was* old, of course, yet Aileen's mother, who was of similar age, always managed to look smart and youthful.

'Yes,' she said. 'It was French this afternoon, and I enjoy that. We're reading *Le Pâtre* at the moment . . .' She stepped forward and instinctively lowered her voice, even though Dr Witherspoon was at the surgery; Grandmother had exceedingly sharp ears. 'Please, have you had a chance to ask Father about Sharon's party yet? I have to let Aileen know tomorrow. We'll get a lift back and we won't be late, I promise.'

Mrs Witherspoon sighed, and brushed a loose strand of hair away from her face. 'I'm sorry, Deborah, but you know your father was on call last night, and he was very tired when he came back from Mr Clancy's. Then this morning your grandmother had some complaints to make. I'll try tonight, after dinner.'

'Thanks, Mother. I know you'll do your best. Where's Henry?'

'I think he's out in the garden. I'll make some tea and – '

The demanding burr of the buzzer cut across her sentence. Although it rang in the kitchen, they could hear the sound clearly through the thin wooden doors of the serving-hatch which linked the kitchen and dining-room.

'I'll go,' said Deborah at once.

'No – I shall,' said her mother grimly, and strode off towards the converted morning-room from where Maud Witherspoon was allowed to rule the entire household.

Deborah stared after her, already feeling downcast, then deposited her briefcase against a chair leg and ran into the garden.

'Henry! Ch-ch-ch-ch,' she called.

At first there was no reply, but the absence of birds near a piece of bread on the lawn meant that he was close at hand.

'I know where you're hiding ... I'm coming to get you!' Deborah edged past the rose-beds towards a particularly large clump of catmint in the herbaceous border. Sure enough, a hint of beige was visible between the abundant stalks of purple flowers.

'Come on, lazy cat,' she said softly, and was rewarded by a slow surge of movement within the clump. With a faint rustle, a large ginger tom emerged, padded towards her, then stopped, arched his back and emitted a ferocious yawn. Deborah crouched down and lovingly stroked the warm fur, feeling the bones of his back beneath her hand, finding the groove between his shoulder blades where pressure was guaranteed to trigger ecstatic purrs.

'Heffalump cat,' she whispered, picking him up and plonking him over her shoulder. She rubbed her face against the silken flank, smelling sunshine, catmint and clean earth. 'Overfed, underexercised ... and all mine.'

She walked back down the lawn, crooning quietly in his ear, then noticed her mother frowning at her through the dining-room window.

'Don't let your father catch you holding Henry like that,' she was told on re-entering the house. 'You know he thinks it's unhealthy.'

With a poor grace Deborah returned her pet to ground level. 'I don't have Father's allergies,' she muttered.

'That's not the point. Cats carry diseases – he'll tell you. We're fortunate he'll let you keep an animal at all.'

'Aileen has two cats, a dog and a guinea-pig.'

'And lives in a little box on the Clarkwood Estate. You have

11

a fine house with an enormous garden, in a lovely village. Be thankful for what you've got.'

Deborah turned away. 'Are *you* thankful, Mother?' she murmured.

Lynn Witherspoon's face tightened ominously. 'Don't be cheeky, Deborah. Go and see to the kettle while I finish here. Mrs Weddell Grant from the Ladies' Friendship Guild is coming to visit your grandmother tonight, and she always manages to engineer a Grand Tour of the premises. Go on, now.'

Deborah went.

'I've brought you some flowers, dear.' Gertrude Weddell Grant bustled into the room with a determined air of ceremony and thrust a straggling bunch of pink carnations at Maud.

'Thank you.' Maud hardly looked at them; her mind was on the greeting she had just received. 'Dear' was a new development, an appellation with sinister undertones. Was she suddenly regarded as senile, or did this overblown woman consider that her illness had reached some sort of preterminal stage where respect was no longer necessary? Whatever the reason, she resented it.

A chair creaked nearby as the vice-president of the LFG lowered herself on to it, and leaned confidentially towards the occupant of the bed. The faint scent of carnation was completely obliterated by perfume waves which would have disgraced an air-freshener spray.

'We all hope you're feeling better, dear,' she began, then launched into the real nitty-gritty. 'We had the annual dinner last night . . . ' She proceeded to itemize the Guild's affairs in mind-numbing detail, scarcely pausing for any 'yes', 'no' or 'really?' to fight its way into a breathing space. This was just as well, since none was forthcoming. Maud watched the woman with concealed contempt; if it wasn't for her own current situation of helplessness, she wouldn't have to suffer the babblings of people like this. It was a high price to pay for

12

company, to be used as a captive audience, then expected to feel grateful at the end of it.

Gertrude Grant (the addition of her maiden name since the death of her husband was pure affectation) was an incorrigible publicity-seeker, one of a growing class of people who seemed to equate publicity with status. Devoid of any specific talent, she had finally found an outlet for her aspirations in charity fund-raising. The LFG, with its vaguely philanthropic constitution had proved the perfect vehicle for collaboration with Hope in the City, a charity which attempted to alleviate hardship among Nottingham's homeless youngsters. Nothing pleased her more than to be photographed by the local press while handing over cheques to the charity; more recently, she had been pictured receiving them, having been made Hope in the City's treasurer. All this would indeed be creditable, thought Maud, except for the near-certainty that any headline-grabbing cause would have engendered equal zeal.

'So, that's a further two hundred pounds for those poor hungry young people,' her visitor was saying. 'There'll be another gala presentation soon. We had a wonderful bequest last week, too, a really generous sum from a lady JP who wrote that she believed our work was God-inspired. I was touched – sorry, have you a cough? As I was saying, I was touched to see that when she realized she had entered her final illness, she turned her thoughts to others outside her immediate family, people not so well provided for. That showed great generosity of spirit.' Her gaze became penetrating, but Maud's silence was a rebuff. 'Anyway, we shall use her gift in the name of benevolence, to clothe the children of the streets and fill their bellies . . .'

'This isn't Calcutta,' snapped Maud, suddenly sick of the syrupy effusion. 'Haven't most of these teenagers deliberately made themselves homeless? And aren't some of them on drugs?'

'Now, dear . . . ' The Weddell Grant shook her head sorrowfully. 'You know that our girls and boys don't all have the parental guidance they deserve. They can make mistakes . . . How *is* young Martin at present? No more – trouble, I hope?'

You fat bitch, thought Maud viciously. A cobra tongue in a

sheep's head. Yet there was a time when she wouldn't have dared. 'That was three years ago,' she said with outward mildness. 'He's a good boy now. A little unconventional for Thorbeck, perhaps, but that's his privilege.'

'I'm sure. Well, it's nice to see you looking – er, it's been nice to see you. Everyone at the Guild sends their best wishes . . . ' She paused as an insolent double rap sounded at the door.

'Come in,' articulated Maud, and a tousle-haired young man entered breezily, wearing a black leather jacket and denim jeans.

'Hi, Gran. I've brought you a scandal sheet. Oh – sorry. Didn't know you had company.' He eyed Mrs Weddell Grant, looked unimpressed, and left again after a few words.

'Such clothes!' chuckled Gertrude with mock indulgence. 'Is he still working among the artisans and riding that bike?'

Maud shared her distaste, but not for anything would she admit it.

'Gertrude – dear,' she said. 'If my roof slates fell off in a storm, I don't think the local accountant would be much use.'

Her attention was briefly held by a small heading in the newspaper which Martin had carelessly thrown across the bed. FAMILY CONTESTS WILL, it proclaimed. Gertrude was spouting something about skilled manual workers being allowed to pay themselves more per hour than a doctor these days. Money . . . yes, that was one thing Maud did have. Money was power. Money made people take notice.

Gertrude had heaved herself off the chair and was hovering gelatinously near the door, having said her piece. Clearly she didn't intend to listen to anything Maud might wish to recount. Maud waited for the valedictions to begin again, then cut firmly across them.

'About that charity of yours,' she said. 'It's true that I've been thinking of my will recently. The family don't need my money: Neville's doing very well at the practice, and he'll look after George. It would be fitting to leave it to a worthy cause. Of course, it's a considerable sum, so I have to be careful about my choice.' She saw an avid look spring into Gertrude's glassy blue eyes. The woman advanced a step, and opened her mouth to gibber.

14

'Bring me some literature about Hope in the City next time you come, will you?' went on Maud. 'It may be a suitable candidate.'

When the door had closed she contemplated the limp carnations, which had dribbled a thin stream of moisture on to the bedspread. Her hand reacted to the irritation by reaching out for the buzzer; her mouth, however, was pulled into a wry twist which might have represented a smile.

2

Dr Neville Witherspoon picked up the next patient record card from his desk and gave a mental groan. Not Harriet Lawson again. Surely it was only ten days since she had last consulted him about a trivial complaint. Irritably he tapped the end of his pen against a nearby dish of paper clips. He tried to be impartial to his patients, as any GP should, to be available to them and allay their fears, real or imaginary. Nevertheless, he was only human, and the mere sight of Harriet Lawson's name made his stomach sink.

Harriet was in her late forties, and unmarried. She had a slender investment inheritance from her mother, but while freely complaining of hardship she felt no urge to find a job. Instead, she spent each day enhancing her reputation as Thorbeck's dark gossip – dark because only tales of illness and misfortune were considered worth passing on, and because her clothes were all of sombre colours.

She had attended the Venning Road surgery for six years now, having left another practice closer to town under some sort of cloud. Neville was well aware of the problems that practice must have experienced; her name now cropped up in his appointments book approximately once a fortnight, and each time the complaint was something ill-defined. She would take up twice the allotted seven minutes, and if a double appointment was booked, that, too, would overrun, to the detriment of others.

Squaring his shoulders, Neville pressed the bell, and moments later the familiar tapping steps sounded outside his door. She knocked; he called 'Come in.'

'How's your throat now, Miss Lawson?' he asked as she sat down. He had learnt the hard way that traditional open-ended questions invited a deluge of irrelevance.

She thrust her pointed chin towards him and opened her mouth wide, as if he could see from across the desk. 'Much better, thank you, with the gargle you recommended. But I've come about something else.'

'Yes?'

'Well, it's . . . *down below* again. My cycles are still irregular. I'm sure there must be something abnormal inside. I wondered if I needed another examination.'

'That isn't necessary, Miss Lawson. You had a very thorough check three weeks ago, and we won't learn anything new.'

'But let me *show* you!'

He started to raise a hand in protest, but subsided when he saw her scrabbling in her capacious black leather handbag. She pulled out a diary and, with a little cough to denote embarrassment, handed it to him; each entry contained lurid descriptions of her erratic menstrual flow, with bizarre attempts to quantify it to the nearest millilitre.

'Yes . . . yes,' he said. 'Remember what we discussed before. It's quite normal for the flow to be irregular at this time.'

'There's the heaviness in the muscles, though, Doctor. It doesn't feel right.'

'The hospital tests you underwent last year excluded any disease,' he said flatly. 'You have nothing to worry about. Just regard these symptoms as a nuisance, nothing more.'

'But what about the hot flushes? They're such a menace. I get them in the post office, and at the hairdresser's, and even when I come in here. They make me feel quite faint.'

'We discussed hormone tablets, didn't we, Miss Lawson? You wanted to think about whether you were going to give them a try. Have you come to any decision?'

'They don't seem quite natural to me.'

Neville waited; he was not going to explain the pros and cons of the therapy for a fourth time.

17

'I'd rather just come and be reassured,' she went on. 'I've got faith in you, Dr Witherspoon. You understand me.'

That was partially true. He knew she was underoccupied, hence her obsession with self; he suspected that for her the surgery represented an important social outlet ... but whether there was any actual, definable mental pathology, he was less sure. Once, he had been driven to write '?Munchausen's Syndrome' in her notes, but had scored through it immediately; it was too facile a pigeon-hole for Harriet, and he knew that true Munchausen's was uncommon.

'*You* understand me,' she persisted.

He felt his skin crawl. There was an ardent gleam in her eye he didn't like.

'Well,' he said briskly, 'if there are no new symptoms, then that's fine. You go away and think about the tablets, and – '

To his astonishment she half-rose, twisted sideways with a little gasp, and slowly unrolled on to the floor. Her precision was miraculous: her shoulders lay two inches from the leg of his desk on one side, and five inches from a filing cabinet on the other.

Frowning, Neville knelt down on the green carpet and felt her carotid pulse. It was strong and regular. Her skin colour was normal. He had little doubt that this was more feint than faint. Unhurriedly he walked to the door and asked Sister Tarrant, the nurse practitioner, if she could spare a moment. 'Miss Lawson has just collapsed,' he said. 'I think she was feeling too warm.'

Sister bustled to help while he wrapped a sphygmomanometer cuff round one of the thin limp arms and went through the motions of taking the blood pressure. Then he withdrew from the situation to watch impassively until Harriet decided it was time to utter a small moan and blink her scanty eyelashes.

By the time his patient was seated, alternately gushing apologies and sipping water from a glass, Neville Witherspoon had made his own decision.

'Miss Lawson,' he said in a father-figure voice borrowed from the senior partner, 'I don't feel you're getting the best service we can offer in routine surgery. Dr Adams has started a Menopause Clinic, which is in session fortnightly on Wednesday evenings, and her expertise could be of great benefit to you. No – hear me out. She's made a special study of all these symptoms which are giving you anxiety, and is in the best position to advise you on ways of alleviating them. Sister, please would you be kind enough to accompany Miss Lawson to Reception, and see that she makes an appointment? Thank you.'

He gave a genial smile, a rare gesture for him, but any feeling of triumph he may have been nurturing was abruptly blighted by Harriet Lawson's reaction. At first she seemed stunned; next, as she backed towards the door, her expression betrayed cheated humiliation. But the look in her eyes which made Neville's skin bunch cold came just as she was leaving. It was pure hostility.

'Neville? Are you busy?' Kenneth Forester, one of the partners, poked his head round the door as the surgery ended.

'Just finishing some paperwork, Ken. Come in.'

The young man strode into the office and sat down on the patients' chair. He wore a red striped shirt with a white collar, a fashion trend Neville personally abhorred, and his shoes were highly polished. He leaned forward, hands loosely clasped together between his knees.

'As you know, Bernard retires in less than three months,' he said. 'I think we need seriously to consider how the work will pan out when he's gone.'

'He'll be missed,' mused Neville. 'The patients adore him, especially elderly ladies and little children. Mother's one of his; she positively blossoms every time he visits. He's one of her own generation who's lived through all the same changes that she has ... I believe my brother George is on his list, too.'

'No, he moved to mine,' said Kenneth. 'Not that I see him often. He usually waits until his asthma is really bad, then comes to me to bail him out. He won't attend routinely. Anyway, about Bernard's retirement – we want the disruption to the practice to be minimal, both from the patients' point of view and our own.'

'It will be. When our trainee starts we'll be kept busy, but after a few weeks he'll be able to share the on-call and generally pull his weight.'

'What about Bernard's pet project, the Child Assessment Clinic, and those other little offices he's always been happy to perform – you know, taking charge of the medical exams for the Red Cross and the St John lot, that kind of thing. Bit of a bore to the rest of us, lurking in some scout hut when the golf course is beckoning!'

'Oh, I'm sure Katherine can handle them.'

'Good. I've had some ideas about the rest . . . ' Kenneth swung one leg over the other and launched into a complex proposal of changes which could be implemented once Bernard Quested had retired. Earnestly he outlined potential new areas of influence for himself, while still paying lip-service to Neville's seniority; the full co-operation of Katherine Adams was taken for granted.

It all sounded well-rehearsed to Neville. Not for the first time his attention was drawn to the paradox of Ken. Ken was only in his late thirties and essentially lazy, yet sometimes he displayed a surprising hunger for status. Neville suspected that the thrusting ambitions of Ken's wife Trudi had a lot to do with his attitude. She was the one who had badgered Ken into joining the golf club because key consultants went there – yet from what Neville had heard, for all Ken's flashy clothes, to describe his golfing performance as mediocre was an act of charity.

Trudi lived vicariously through Ken, and Neville knew by instinct that she longed to see her own husband's name at the top of the brass plate: such extra kudos among her friends! But neither Trudi nor Ken could alter the conventions within the surgery. Primordiality was all; Neville's accession to the senior partner's chair – and with it the largest office – was secure.

*

20

In the corridor outside, Katherine Adams had been standing with her hand stretched out towards the door handle of Neville's office. She hadn't intended to eavesdrop, but the door was slightly open and the sound of her own name, uttered with such cavalier complacency, had given her involuntary pause. A few seconds were enough to convey the gist of the conversation, and when she forced herself to withdraw she could feel the indignation burning high on her cheeks.

She strode into the Rest Room where Sister Tarrant was chatting cosily with the chiropodist, and a medical student on rotation from Sherwood University was sipping his coffee. Each of them smiled or nodded a greeting at her as she helped herself from the percolator.

'I'm afraid Dr Witherspoon has managed to palm off Miss Lawson on to your Wednesday clinic,' said Sister apologetically.

'I know – his Munchausen. I've just come from Reception. He might have asked me first.'

'What's a Munchausen?' enquired the chiropodist, a plump, capable lady who did peripatetic sessions for the whole district.

'You explain, Jonathan,' Katherine invited.

The student was eager to show off his knowledge. 'It's a syndrome where the patients pop up at hospitals or GP surgeries with all manner of symptoms, and willingly undergo investigations, even invasive ones. They tell lies, they often induce their own physical signs, and the condition is essentially psychiatric.' He smiled. 'It's named after an eighteenth-century German baron, and is known colloquially among medics as the "Undhier" syndrome: *hier*, und *hier*, und *hier* . . .' He clapped a hand to various parts of his anatomy while pulling his face into a range of agonized expressions; the chiropodist guffawed with laughter.

'Do you really think she's a Munchausen, Dr Adams?' asked Sister Tarrant.

'No; it's a tempting label, but from the notes I've seen, Miss Lawson would balk at unnecessary surgery. At worst she's borderline. True Munchausens take their deceptions to extremes, and end up criss-crossed with scars.'

'Some, even have amputations they don't need,' said Jonathan ghoulishly, and this time the chiropodist shuddered.

Katherine sat back and drank her coffee, reflecting on the morning's events. Of course she could cope with another difficult patient, despite her busy list; she hadn't practised medicine for over twenty years to shy away from its more demanding aspects. But she was angry with Neville. His action was symptomatic of the general attitude to her taken by the two younger partners: anything unpopular with them, she would handle. Family planning, women's health screening, antenatal checks, menopausal problems – these were a woman's province. Now, it seemed, they hoped to ease the Child Assessment Clinic into her sphere of jurisdiction, after years of grandfatherly supervision by Bernard Quested.

Why shouldn't Neville do it? He had solid experience of fatherhood ... Children had once been so important to him that he had adopted one of his own.

Trudi Forester dropped a slice of lemon into her martini and stirred the clinking ice with a cocktail stick.

'You mustn't miss this opportunity, Ken,' she pronounced. 'With Bernard gone, you can expand, take on more responsibilities. Don't let Neville run everything.'

'Don't worry,' he said. 'I know how to carve out a niche for myself. I shan't sink into the background.'

'I should think not! You deserve recognition, but with Neville in the way you won't be senior partner for years! Imagine if he hangs on till he's seventy, like Bernard; you'll be knocking on sixty yourself. It doesn't seem fair. He's so stodgy and conservative. He just knows the right people, sits on committees and talks. But *you* come up with all the progressive ideas that get the practice noticed.'

Kenneth Forester gave a wry smile. Much as he would have liked to believe that Trudi's main concern was for his job satisfaction, he knew her far too well for that. No, Trudi was avid for social standing. Most of the 'progressive ideas' had been her own; once she had even tried to encourage him to

22

become a media doctor, with a magazine column and a spot on local radio, but he finally found an effective deterrent: one mention of the word 'downmarket' and she dropped the idea from her jaws as if it were impregnated with Angostura bitters.

Nevertheless, Trudi's hawkish qualities suited him. At least she was intelligent, and keen to discuss medicopolitical matters such as budgeting considerations and the organization of the Health Service. At formal dinners she took care to woo any hospital consultant in a position of influence, and they were invariably charmed by her. She contrasted so obviously with Neville's dull wife Lynn, who scarcely had a word to say for herself.

'Do you think Judge Atherton will be transferred to your list?' she went on eagerly. 'You must suggest it to Bernard – subtly, of course.'

'Trudi, it's for him to recommend.'

'I appreciate that, but if he doesn't know you're interested, he'll probably pass the judge on to Neville. What about the Medical Society? There'll be a vacant seat. Someone will have to nominate you . . . ' She continued in this vein for some minutes, then returned to her original grumble. 'It's a great pity Neville isn't older.'

'He isn't, though. Would you like me to pull out and start my own practice? Put the house on the line, go back to near-perpetual on-call?' He spoke teasingly, but with an edge.

'No! We've had enough of that.'

'I agree. So short of a scandal, Neville will be head of the practice for the next fifteen years, and that's that.'

'Scandal!' She pulled a face. 'He's so boring, dutiful and positively *Victorian*, you'd never find a whiff of scandal near him! Unless you count that episode with Martin.'

'I'm going to watch the news,' said Ken. He drained his glass of whisky, picked up the television's remote control and activated the set to catch the seven o'clock news. The first item concerned the national economy, a subject which normally fascinated Trudi, but this time her sharp comments were in abeyance. She was quiet and thoughtful, her perfect profile smooth as glass.

Plotting, thought Ken.

3

Lynn was waiting for Neville with unaccustomed fire in her eyes when he arrived home from evening surgery on Friday.

'I must speak with you,' she hissed, hanging his coat on a sturdy brass hook.

He clamped down on a reflex wave of annoyance. After a tiring surgery peppered with niggling administrative problems, the last thing he wanted was involvement in domestic unrest. Lynn was a quiet, accepting, almost stolid woman – some of the reasons he had married her – but when she was stirred to anger, her passions were all the more intense for having been held in check. Such exhibitions were distasteful to him.

'It's about Maud . . .'

'The dining-room,' he said tersely. He led the way in silence, straight-backed despite his fatigue, and they took up positions across the table which Deborah had laid for dinner.

'Where are the children?' he asked.

'In their rooms, I think. Or the garden. Neville, Harriet Lawson caught me outside the baker's today.'

'Yes?' He spoke coolly, but he was apprehensive. Had the damned woman complained?

'She was eager to talk, which isn't like her. Usually she ignores me. She said . . . ' Lynn flushed with fury. 'She said that Maud is going to make a new will, cutting out all the family – George, the children, everyone. The money is to go to that pet charity of Gertrude's: Hope in the City. Neville, it's monstrous!' For a moment his mind reeled; he had expected to hear something quite different. Then he experienced relief.

'Harriet Lawson is having you on,' he said with a pale smile. 'That woman is a born trouble-maker. It probably amuses her to spread ridiculous tales like this.'

'It's not ridiculous,' said Lynn thickly. 'She was *specific*. Three of her acquaintances have been invited to be witnesses; there's going to be some sort of ceremony next Thursday in Maud's room. I – I had to pretend I knew, to save face, but – Neville, what's going on?'

'How should I know?' he snapped, feeling irritated again. 'Perhaps it's some game of Mother's, but I can hardly ask her in order to find out, can I?'

Lynn looked down at her hands as they gripped the back of a dining chair; ridges of work-dry skin retracted from the jutting ivory knuckles.

'Why not?' she asked, quivering with the effort to stay calm.

'Why not? It simply isn't done!'

She gaped at him. '*Not done*? How convenient for her. Well, I'll tell you what I think. I think it *isn't done* to sponge off your son's family for eight long years, then pull a trick like this! It's not the humiliation that I mind, although the thought of the entire LFG gossiping about this doesn't exactly fill me with joy; I suppose I should be used to it by now. No, it's the idea of her playing cat and mouse with the children's inheritance! You and I agreed long ago that we didn't want anything from her ourselves, but we can't stand by and let the children be robbed!'

'Keep your voice down!' he ordered, suddenly aware of noises on the far side of the serving-hatch which led from the kitchen. 'Mother's money is her own concern,' he went on more quietly. 'I have no intention of discussing it with her, or anyone else.'

'But she's *using* us,' persisted Lynn. 'Haven't we a right to know where we stand?'

As always, when Neville found himself faced with conflicting loyalties, he retreated into a cold shell.

'That's enough,' he said. 'I won't hear any more. This subject is closed.'

It was a time-honoured formula of his, one which brooked no argument, but just to underline the point he sat down,

25

opened his briefcase and began to leaf through the papers inside.

White-lipped, Lynn left the room.

Deborah checked the hem of her dress in the mirror, picked up her jacket and bag, then moved to the bed.

'Time to go,' she whispered to Henry, who was doing his orange dralon cushion impersonation.

He stared at her solemnly with large golden eyes, then let the lids slowly fall again.

'Come on,' she said, scooping him up. 'Father musn't find you here.'

No, indeed. There was an 'atmosphere' in the house this evening, not an unusual occurrence, but one which made circumspection advisable. At breakfast Father had agreed to take her to Aileen's on his way to a meeting; from there Aileen's father would escort the girls to and from the party. Deborah was loath to jeopardize this rare concession.

As she closed the door of her small bedroom another door opened opposite and Martin sauntered out on to the landing. Henry dug in his claws, struggled free and ran down the stairs.

'You off out?' Martin asked his sister.

'Yes; a party. Sharon from school.'

'Pink frilly dresses and pass the parcel?' he sneered.

'Don't be silly, Martin.'

'I'm not. That's what Father would like to think, isn't it? All little girls together, and home by eleven.' He looked at her shrewdly. 'Perhaps it'll be your lucky night and this Sharon knows where it's at. Maybe you'll be smoking grass and getting laid.'

Deborah felt her neck burn. She hated it when he spoke like that, or used even coarser figures of speech absorbed from the building site where he worked. What had started as an act of rebellion against their parents was now engrained, and Martin was fast becoming a stranger.

'I'm fifteen,' she murmured, then hurried on before he

26

could offend her again. 'What about you? You're looking smart – are you going to the club?'

'Yep.'

He swaggered down the stairs behind her, stylish in a light beige suit. Tonight he even wore a tie, and the whole ensemble represented a marked contrast to his daytime Levis and leathers.

Their parents were in the kitchen, suspended in a strained silence which Martin affected not to notice.

'If Beverley rings,' he called out casually to his mother, 'will you tell her I'm not around? Say I've gone on an overland trek to Pakistan, or something.'

Lynn shook her head. 'No, I won't. You've been stringing that little girl along for years, so if you've any bad news for her, you must tell her yourself.'

'I've tried to. She won't take no for an answer.'

'Then you'll have to be more persuasive. I'll take messages, but I won't lie for you.'

He shrugged and went out by the kitchen door, whereupon Neville stepped over to join Deborah.

'Are you ready?' he asked.

She nodded.

'Let me see your bag.'

She held it out, her heart already thudding uncomfortably.

'Show me the inside, please.' Deborah undid the main zip and waited while he probed the feminine paraphernalia within.

'I'm glad to see there's no make-up. You know I forbid it . . . There *is* no make-up, is there?' He looked her in the face, and she couldn't frame the lie. 'Deborah?'

She hung her head so that the mid-length mousy hair swung forward to cover her shame.

'Give it to me.'

With trembling fingers she tugged at the discreetly positioned side zip and brought out the glossy pink lipstick she had bought with such pleasure that day at the chemist's. She placed it on his outstretched palm and watched as he turned and threw it into the Aga. Now the lecture would start . . .

Mercifully, it never materialized. Perhaps her father was

27

just tired, or perhaps he had other things on his mind. Whatever the reason, he contented himself with one short, hurtful observation: 'Sometimes you disappoint me, Deborah,' before they walked mutely to the car together, leaving Lynn Witherspoon alone with her mother-in-law and the buzzer.

'Hurry, Aileen! It's a quarter to eleven!'

'Seems a pity to spoil my handiwork,' said Aileen, hovering with a lotion-soaked ball of cotton wool near Deborah's left cheek. 'Have a last look,' she suggested, holding up a mirror.

Deborah couldn't resist. Three hours earlier Aileen had transformed her ordinary, schoolgirl face into something stunning. She had felt like a new person at the party, someone lively, interesting and sought-after. Certainly not that gauche teenager, Deborah Witherspoon. It was as if the make-up was an actor's mask which hid her true insignificance and allowed her to adopt whatever role seemed appropriate in the circumstances; it freed her from herself.

'You look about twenty,' commented Aileen.

Shadowed eyelids ... cheek-bones sculpted with blusher ... lips the colour of cranberries, moistly gleaming in the side-light of a nearby shaded lamp...

'Yes,' agreed Deborah, absurdly gratified.

Abruptly she pulled away from the mirror and allowed Aileen to destroy the illusion with swift, competent strokes of cleanser.

'Your brother looks older than he is, as well,' went on Aileen. 'What is he now, eighteen? I wish you'd introduce me to some of his friends.'

'You wouldn't like them,' said Deborah. She didn't. Since his mid-teens Martin had determinedly consorted with the same rough individuals who had introduced him to bikes and leathers, under-age drinking in spit-and-sawdust pubs, amusement arcades, foul-smelling cigarettes and bleached, common little girl friends like Beverley. The only example of their macho stigmata he had so far eschewed was that irreversible horror, the tattoo. Yet perhaps there was hope ...

more recently, since he had discovered a particular nightclub, Martin had begun to dress more smartly in the evenings. Perhaps one phase of his adolescent rebellion was coming to an end.

Deborah snatched up her bag and prepared to dash down the stairs to Mr Blanchard, who was waiting to take her home in his car.

'Thanks for everything, Aileen,' she said, her eyes wistfully scanning the happy clutter of her friend's room.

'Here,' said Aileen, holding out a pile of *Ginette*, a popular teenage magazine.

'Oh – I can't.' *Ginette*, like all the others, was forbidden.

''Course you can.' Aileen deftly peeled off the top few copies, rolled them into a cylinder and stuffed them into the sleeve of Deborah's jacket. 'See,' she said. 'It's easy. Just carry that under your arm.'

Deborah hesitated, then picked up the jacket as though it were china. She still found deception hard.

It was a great relief to find that Father's car was still absent from the drive. Thanking Mr Blanchard, Deborah ran lightly in through the unlocked kitchen door; muffled noises came from the adjoining utility room, so she was able to creep upstairs and hide the magazines before making her presence known.

Mother obviously hadn't heard her come in. She was leaning over the sink, scrubbing vigorously at a soiled sheet with a special bar of soap which helped to remove stains. Seen in profile, her face was tense, the jaw clenched, a frown pushing her forehead into ridges. Unsure what to do, Deborah gave a small cough.

Lynn Witherspoon swung round, and her expression of stark fury made Deborah quail. Instantly it faded, but it was already too late.

'You startled me,' she said. 'Your grandmother spilt tea on this sheet and I was just trying to stop the stain taking hold.'

She turned off the running tap. 'Did you have a nice time at the party?'

'Yes.'

Her mother came closer. 'You've still got some eyeliner on; better get rid of that before your father arrives.'

'Yes,' said Deborah sullenly. Then, 'Why?'

'Why what?'

'Why *aren't* I allowed to wear make-up? All the other girls do. It isn't fair.'

'Your father would say that you don't need it, and young skin is pretty enough on its own. But I think he's also afraid that you'll attract boys, and be distracted from your studies just when it's important to apply yourself.'

'Then why doesn't he tell me that, instead of issuing rules and orders? Why doesn't he explain?'

Lynn smiled ruefully. 'Your father's never been any good at explaining things. We have to accept that that's how he is. But I promise you that any rules he makes are because he loves you and wants the best for you.'

'I feel so different,' muttered Deborah, before taking the offensive again. 'What about Martin? Why is he allowed to do as he pleases, go where he likes – come home at all hours?'

A curious blankness stilled Lynn Witherspoon's features. 'Martin's older than you are,' she said mechanically.

'He always has been. But I'm fifteen now, and when he was fifteen he wasn't restricted as I am. In fact, that was when – '

'That's enough, Deborah. Go and wash your face while I finish here.'

As her daughter slouched morosely out of the room, Lynn spared her no more thought. She was intent on rubbing and pummelling the sheet, a new white one which she had allocated to Maud with some reluctance. Now it was permanently marked.

She couldn't rid herself of the idea that Maud had done it deliberately. There had been something in the old lady's eyes tonight – a malicious, knowing look, a challenge even – which had triggered sick fury in Lynn. That harridan knew the basic helplessness of her daughter-in-law's position, the fact that Neville assiduously avoided taking sides and tried to pretend unpleasantness didn't exist. She knew that the family had left Lynn alone – again. She had decided to amuse herself.

Lynn raised the affected portion of the sheet and wrung it out savagely, as if it were Maud's scrawny neck. That spiteful old hag and her games. She had manipulated the family for years – and now suddenly her very will was in question. Lynn didn't share Neville's dissociated optimism that Harriet Lawson had got her facts wrong. It would be just like Maud to alter the will with a grand flourish, ensure the fluttering gratitude of the LFG, then later, when she was tired of them, consider changing it again. Perhaps her family would be reinstated – but when? Supposing she became too frail, or died too soon?

I don't want her money, thought Lynn. To me, everything of hers is tainted. But it's the children's birthright. How many years of uncertainty do we have to endure? How many more years of *this*?

Her chapped hands squeezed water from the sheet again, and slowly she became aware that someone nearby was reciting a monotonous litany:

'Why doesn't she just die? I could kill her myself . . . I could kill her myself . . . '

It was a shock to find that the voice was her own.

4

'Well, Maud, how are you today?'

Maud sat as straight as she could in bed, scented with lavender water and wearing a clean night-gown. Dr Quested's visits were always both a pleasure and a pain: he was a gentleman, with courtesy to match, a quality she was convinced was becoming extinct, yet he was also her doctor, and Maud suffered a Victorian reticence about discussing any symptoms she regarded as embarrassing.

'Holding my own,' she said stoutly. 'There's life in the old girl yet.'

'So I should hope. We intend to get you up and around again when your joints are feeling a little better. How are the knees?'

'Stiff, but not too painful. I'm afraid this wrist lets me down, though . . . ' (That humiliating episode with the tea last week. But she would *not* descend to using a feeding-cup!)

'Let me see.' He gently felt the swollen joint, and Maud grimaced against her will.

'My fingers,' she said hastily. 'Not much of a sight now, are they? I won't be wearing rings again.'

Lightly he touched her left forefinger, which was deformed by subluxation at the first joint. 'The textbooks compare this with a swan's neck,' he smiled, 'and I can think of nothing more graceful.'

'Flattery!' she chided. 'But at my age it's welcome. Do you remember the piano I used to have at Larchbank? The baby grand I played every day?'

'I do indeed. Your recitals were the joy of the neighbourhood . . . '

For a short time they spoke reminiscently of Chopin waltzes
and customs from a bygone era, then Dr Quested steered the
conversation back to his patient's health.

'How is the dyspepsia you mentioned last time? Is the white
medicine helping?'

'A little,' she said. 'Just a little.'

'Has the pain in your stomach got worse?'

'Well . . . a little.'

'Hmm. Your tablets have probably been irritating the stomach lining. I think we must adjust the dose and give you bland
foods at present. Perhaps you'd better leave the sherry alone
for a few days, too.'

'Oh . . . what a pity. I have some friends coming on Thursday for a special party. May I not have just one small glass?'

'A very small one, if you insist. Now if there's nothing else
causing you discomfort, I shall go and talk to your daughter-
in-law about how best to take care of you.'

Lynn ushered the elderly GP into the lounge, and tried to look
alert while he delivered a series of instructions for the general
cosseting of Maud.

'What is actually wrong with her?' she asked politely.
'Apart from the rheumatoid arthritis, that is.'

'I believe it's gastritis,' he said. 'An irritation of the stomach
lining. Or possibly an ulcer is developing. This can happen
with steroid drugs, and I shall tail them down immediately.
She should stop taking the other tablets altogether, and take
these new ones I'm prescribing. On no account give her aspirins.' A door banged at the side of the house. 'Ah, is that
Neville? I'll explain the situation to him as well.'

He gave Lynn a little bow and twinkled at her.

'Maud is very lucky to have you,' he said.

'Deborah . . . '

Deborah halted outside the school gates and looked about

33

her for the source of the voice. Aileen was staying on for her Friday tennis coaching, so she was alone.

'Deborah . . . '

Now she could see who it was. A short girl with skinny legs under a crumpled yellow miniskirt advanced hesitantly towards her. Her hair was bleached and her pink frosted nails were bitten.

'Hello, Beverley,' she said slowly. She wondered what Martin's former girl friend could possibly want with her. They had never got on. ('Hi, Debs.' 'My name is Deborah.')

'Can yer do us a favour?' the girl asked.

'What is it?'

Beverley fidgeted. From a distance of two feet, she looked pale and ill. 'I've got ter see Martin, but 'e won't ring me and 'e won't come round. Can you ask 'im ter ring? It's important.'

'I can ask,' said Deborah doubtfully, 'but he seems to be busy most evenings.'

'Is 'e goin' wi' someone?' Beverley's bitten nails were clenched into her palms and her face looked more pinched than ever.

'I think it's just the boys,' said Deborah. She wasn't sure; she suspected he had met a new girl at the club.

'Will yer tell 'im anyway?'

'Yes.' Deborah glanced at her watch. She would miss the school bus if she didn't hurry.

'Please – yer will, won't yer?' Beverley was reaching out as if to detain her.

'I said I would.'

Deborah was surprised to see her mother hurrying across the greensward when she alighted at Thorbeck half an hour later. It was rare for Grandmother to be left alone in the afternoons; perhaps a friend was with her – or had something happened?

She called out and her mother paused, breathless and agitated.

'Hello, darling,' she said as Deborah approached. 'I

34

just popped out to the shop. What sort of day have you had?'

'The usual.' Deborah fell into step with her. 'What did you buy?'

Lynn's gaze flickered to the slender handbag which was all that she carried. 'Oh – I went to the post office section; just a few stamps. We'll get our groceries tomorrow, at Sainsbury's.'

There was no further conversation as they turned into the cul-de-sac; neither of them had anything she wished to say. Deborah was moodily aware that the tense atmosphere which had hung over the house since the departure of three elderly ladies the previous evening was unlikely to be soon dispelled. Only the sight of a neighbour's black cat lifted her spirits a notch; she would play 'string' with Henry in the garden when she reached her own home.

All was quiet as her mother unlocked the kitchen door and led the way inside. Father was doing house calls, Martin was up on one of his roofs; Grandmother's buzzer remained silent. She paused as Lynn began to fill the kettle from the tap.

'Can I have my tea in a few minutes, please?' she asked. 'I want to find Henry first.'

'Whatever you like,' Lynn replied, 'but I'd be obliged if you'd check on your grandmother before you do.'

Deborah groaned. 'Do I *have* to?'

'Yes. She hasn't rung this afternoon, so I haven't disturbed her. She's bound to want something by now.'

Grumbling, Deborah left the kitchen and walked down the gloomy inner passageway which led to 'Grandmother's sitting-room', the chamber where Maud was now bedridden.

She tapped once; no imperious voice called for her to enter. She tapped again, waited, then cautiously turned the handle and stepped inside.

The bed was awash with red. Blood had saturated the counterpane and spread out like the petals of some sinister mutant amaryllis, a scarlet monster whose thirst for growth had sucked its begetter dry.

Maud Witherspoon was a lifeless husk, hunched so small and pale in all that vibrant colour that she seemed an irrelevance. It took effort to study her rather than the bed, to follow

35

the rusty trail from the slack old mouth, and notice that in
death the hands were curiously graceful as they lay palms up,
appealing for help that never came.

5

'Listen to this one, Will!' Inspector Richard Montgomery of Nottinghamshire's CID gave a rare chuckle as his sergeant walked into the office. He had been sorting through the morning's mail, sifting out priority items, when he had come across an anonymous typed letter.

'*Dear Inspector Montgomery,*' he read, '*I hesitate to bother you, but the man at number 26 Acacia Crescent has been claiming unemployment benefit for nearly a year while working as a painter and decorator. He also obtained insurance money for the rebuilding of a fence after last month's storms, when in fact there was never a fence there before. It really is a disgrace, with honest citizens going short. I hope you'll do something about it.*' Montgomery raised his head. 'He's put *c.c. Inland Revenue, DSS and Royal Indemnity*, just for good measure.'

'I can sympathize with that,' said William Bird. 'Types like the one he describes often brag about their petty frauds, which must gall their neighbours no end.'

'This writer will be a pensioner and male,' divined Montgomery. 'I wonder why such letters keep coming to me?'

'Fame. People pick up your name from their local papers . . . Funnily enough, I was just bringing you a strange letter myself.'

'You'd better have a seat.'

'Thanks.' Sergeant Bird eased his stout body on to a chair, produced a blue envelope which was slit across the top, and extracted a sheet of matching blue paper. 'This was just addressed to "The Police",' he said. 'It says: *To whom it may concern. Maud Witherspoon did not die naturally. It's all because of*

37

the money. No signature.' He handed the sheet to Montgomery, who took it carefully.

'Hmm. Maud Witherspoon. Is the name supposed to mean anything?'

'It doesn't to me. We could check among the registered deaths, of course, but is it worth the time? This is probably some silly hoax.'

Montgomery was looking at the envelope. It had been posted in central Nottingham, which gave little away. First-class stamp. Address same handwriting as the letter.

He sucked in his cheeks doubtfully. 'Let's just run the most basic of checks,' he said. 'You never know.'

Maud Witherspoon turned out to be an elderly lady who had died from a gastrointestinal haemorrhage two weeks before. The signature, *B. E. Quested*, on the death certificate, seemed familiar to Montgomery. After some thought he recalled that it was the name of the principal at the group practice his wife Carole attended.

For this reason Montgomery himself drove into the car park of Venning Road Health Centre the next morning to make general enquiries; he didn't want a detective constable with two left feet upsetting everyone.

'Dr Quested will see you shortly,' he was told at Reception. 'He's engaged at the moment. Would you like to sit on the chair just outside his room?'

There was a murmuring within as Montgomery waited, then the door opened and a smart, dark-suited young man emerged, still talking.

'. . . read our literature, you'll find that the trials bear out all I've told you. Nice to have met you, Dr Quested.'

'Good day.' This mellower voice belonged to an elderly gentleman with shortsighted eyes and a benign face, who turned to Montgomery and ushered him into the office.

'Yet another antidepressant on the market,' he said with a wry smile, indicating a packet labelled 'Physician's sample' on the desk. 'Better than all the others, of course – the trials say so. Trials sponsored by the drug company. In case I should forget the name of the pill they give me presents. Don't worry – no cars or trips abroad. Just these.'

Montgomery saw a logo-printed notepad and a small egg-cup-shaped receptacle filled with paper clips.

'They don't influence your prescribing, then?' he asked.

'Good Lord, no. I've been prescribing some of the same drugs for the last forty years! Just a moment . . . ' He pottered to a low cupboard alongside one wall, opened it and tossed the sample inside. Montgomery was just in time to see the threatened avalanche of similar packets before the door was closed again.

'Now, what can I do for you, Inspector?'

They sat down at opposite sides of the desk.

'Maud Witherspoon,' said Montgomery.

'Yes?' The GP's expression was merely expectant.

'I believe you were her attendant physician during her last illness.'

'A lot longer than that, I assure you. Maud and I go back – went back – nearly half a century.'

'Did you consider that there was anything suspicious about the death?'

Dr Quested looked amazed. 'No. I wouldn't have signed the certificate if I had. Why do you ask?'

'The question has been raised.'

'I can't imagine why. Who would say such a thing?'

'Tell me about her illness and why she died.'

Dr Quested settled in his chair. 'Maud had rheumatoid arthritis,' he said. 'It came on late in life, and took a rapid course. She had specialist care at the hospital, and all the treatments one would deem it reasonable to try for a lady of her years, but the disease progressed inexorably. It doesn't just affect joints, you know, but other organs including the gut. The stomach lining can become thinned and liable to bleed. Pain-relieving tablets can also affect the stomach and provoke ulcers.

'Latterly, Maud had been suffering from abdominal pain. We didn't want to put her through the discomforts of a barium meal examination or gastroscopy at the hospital; she was too frail. So we treated her on the assumption that an ulcer or gastritis was developing, and adjusted her medication accordingly. Unfortunately she had a massive bleed and died.'

'Natural causes, then.'

'Yes.'

'You said, "*we* treated her", Dr Quested . . . '

'That's right. She was my patient, but of course I discussed every aspect of treatment strategy with her son Neville, who is a partner here.'

'Ah!' Montgomery had noticed that 'Witherspoon' had been second of the four names engraved on the surgery's brass plate. 'I'd like to speak to him, too, if it's convenient.'

'I'll introduce you.'

Neville Witherspoon had a cool, dry handshake and a humourless face. He wore a grey suit and seemed to be about fifty years of age.

'This is very obscure,' he said to Montgomery when Dr Quested had left them alone together. 'Why should anyone send you a note querying Mother's death? Perhaps a haemorrhage sounds dramatic to people who don't understand these things.'

'Were you satisfied with the way Dr Quested was looking after her?'

'Oh yes. He'd been her GP for many years, and I've always admired his management in cases of elderly patients with chronic disease. He kept me in the picture, and I agreed with his decisions.'

'You didn't feel there was any need for a post-mortem?'

An irritated frown flitted across the doctor's forehead. 'No. Mother's death was consistent with her condition, and she had been well attended throughout.'

Montgomery nodded. 'The question of the money was raised,' he said after a pause.

Neville Witherspoon flushed unattractively. 'So that's it,' he said.

'You think that's the reason we were petitioned?'

'Bound to be – but they're wasting their time.'

Montgomery groped for enlightenment. 'Tell me exactly what happened,' he suggested.

40

'You probably know most of it. Her will favoured my brother George and my two children, Martin and Deborah. We all approved this arrangement; my wife Lynn and I are comfortably off. However, shortly before her death Mother altered her own copy of the will, indicating that she wanted to leave the bulk of the estate to a charity. This new provision was witnessed, but turned out to be invalid legally, because she wrote her statement *below* the signatures. The solicitor's copy remained unchanged.'

'So the original will stands?'

'Yes. It had expressed her intentions accurately for fourteen years.'

'What did you make of the attempted alteration?'

The doctor pursed his lips. 'I have an opinion, Inspector,' he said slowly, 'but I'm reluctant to divulge it.'

'This isn't a game.'

'That's where you may be wrong. All right, then . . . I think Mother was guilty of mischief. The charity which would have benefited is closely associated with Mrs Weddell Grant, a woman she never got on with; to me it's inconceivable that Mother would have wished them to have her money.'

'Could she have been coerced?'

'No. Her body might have been worn out, but her brain was like a machete.'

'Who was her solicitor?'

'Mr Barton, of Barton and Mehrs.'

'Thank you.' Storm in a teacup, thought Montgomery. Someone was just expressing their resentment in a tangible form, probably the charity woman. It would all simmer down. Nevertheless, he would complete his one-man investigation now he had got this far.

'Were you as a family aware that your mother was going to change her will?'

'Yes.'

'Did anyone believe she meant it?'

'It seemed unlikely.'

'Do you think she was teasing you, as well?'

'It's possible.'

'How long after the will was altered did she die?'

41

'Er – the following day.' Dr Witherspoon's little *moue* of discomfort seemed entirely appropriate in the circumstances.

'*The following day?*'

'Yes.'

'I see.' A dodgy will; natural causes; doctors ... Montgomery found himself unusually indecisive.

'Concern was expressed to us anonymously,' he reiterated with care. 'Can you think of anyone apart from Mrs Weddell Grant who might want to cause trouble for you or your family?'

'Any of those cats at the LFG is capable.'

'I beg your pardon?'

'Sorry – that's the Ladies' Friendship Guild, a village society which used to be respectable. Both Mother and Lynn have been members in their time. But now, it's a hotbed of gossip, and the wrong types have clawed their way to positions of prominence ... Mrs Weddell Grant is on their committee, and Hope in the City is their adopted charity.'

'We're really looking for someone with a more specific grudge.'

The word 'grudge' appeared to trigger a flash of comprehension in Neville Witherspoon's eyes. He took a deep breath, but stayed silent.

'You have an idea?' asked Montgomery.

'I thought I did, but – no. I can't say.'

On impulse, Montgomery revealed a small portion of the letter, but the doctor shook his head.

'I've never seen that writing before,' he said.

Montgomery stowed it away philosophically. 'Let's hope we don't see it again.'

As they left the office, a woman came out of a door further up the corridor and gave them a brief half-smile before entering a small room opposite. She had smooth, mid-length brown hair gathered into a bun at the nape of her neck, and good legs, Montgomery noticed. The dangling stethoscope showed that she belonged to the practice. He glanced at the door-plate as he passed, and read 'Dr Katherine Adams'. So that was Carole's doctor! Clearly brains were sometimes allowed to coexist with beauty.

He had to force himself to concentrate on the name of the solicitor he was about to visit.

'Mrs Witherspoon's actions were most irregular,' said Mr Barton. 'If she had wanted to make a valid change to her will, her best course was to revoke the previous one and make an entirely new one. Instead, she attempted to revise her own copy.'

'I understand the procedure was witnessed,' murmured Montgomery.

'Oh, yes; that part was carefully done. But the signatures came between her statement of intention to change and the paragraph detailing the new beneficiary – namely, the charity Hope in the City. For obvious reasons, no legacy appearing below a testator's signature can be considered valid.'

'And she hadn't mentioned this to you at all?'

'No; I was most surprised. I'm her executor as well as the family solicitor, and she'd discussed trust funds for the grandchildren with me on more than one occasion . . . Well, as it is, the original will stands – and I have to say I think natural justice has prevailed.'

Angela Cording hurried across Nottingham's market square towards the bench which had just been vacated. Markets were never held here now, but it was a pleasant open space right in the city centre where people could rest amidst flowers and fountains. Her bags were heavy; she wanted to check each purchase against her shopping list before taking the shuttle bus back to the car park.

Someone else appeared to be aiming for the same bench, but never mind – there was room for two. As Angela assessed the seat for sticky marks or pigeon droppings, she suddenly realized that the other woman seemed familiar.

'Lynn!' she exclaimed.

'Angela – hello. How are you?'

They sat down, and Angela lifted the shopping bag on to the wooden slats beside her. 'I'm fine, thank you,' she replied. 'I've been buying some birthday presents for Ruth's twins . . . You look marvellous, Lynn.' As soon as the words were out she felt a stab of embarrassment. Hadn't there just been a death in the family? But then Lynn never had got on well with old Maud Witherspoon. Three years before, when they had been neighbours, both Lynn and Deborah had treated Angela as something of a confidante. But since the Witherspoons had moved to Thorbeck, she had seen relatively little of them, just the odd glimpse of Lynn in town, looking worn and preoccupied, her skin and hair neglected. Now she seemed transformed.

Lynn smiled. 'It's kind of you to say so. I've been to the hairdresser's. I wasn't sure what I wanted, but they've put in some highlights, and I don't think it's too bad at all.'

'It suits you,' said Angela sincerely. 'Where are you off to now? Shall we have a quick cup of coffee somewhere?'

'I'd like that, but perhaps another day. I'm just on my way to look at a job. The opticians on Farrier's Row have advertised for a receptionist. Part time; it sounded ideal.'

'That's great! I hope it's a nice place, and they offer the job to you.' Welcome back to the land of the living, she almost added, and the sentiment reminded her of Maud Witherspoon. She ought to be mentioned, however briefly.

Lynn was rising to her feet and smoothing down the skirt of her pale primrose suit. 'I'm afraid I have to go now,' she said.

'Tell Neville I'm sorry about his mother,' blurted out Angela.

'I will.'

Lynn's expression had immediately become distant. With a murmured 'goodbye' she swung round and walked across the square in new shoes, altering course only to avoid the pigeons pecking near her feet.

Angela stared after her. No confidences this time, she thought; behind the gay trappings she had touched a psyche grown odd and impenetrable. Her newborn optimism for Lynn's future perished in its chrysalis.

'You're going out!' Montgomery's tone held some surprise.

His wife Carole winked at him. 'Top marks for your shimmering deductive powers,' she said. 'I *did* put it on the calendar, but you've obviously forgotten.'

'Am I expected?'

'Not unless you've had a sudden sex change. No – it's the LFG. Joan has twisted my arm to go to another meeting with her as a kind of probationary member. I can tell already that it's not quite my scene, but I promised I would give it a fair trial.' She moved to the wall mirror and drew a comb through her glossy dark hair in brisk strokes. 'I'm picking Joan up in the Mini.'

'Enjoy yourself.' That was more than a platitude; already Montgomery was considering Carole for possible fifth-column duties. 'What is tonight's subject?'

'Local History and Ancient Ruins. Go on, comment.'

'Do I need to?'

She made a face at him and whirled out of the door.

45

6

'I have something rather unpleasant to tell you.'

Neville Witherspoon's family looked at him warily from their positions around the dinner table. Lynn was usually chosen as the conduit for unwelcome information; Neville preferred to remain a remote figure on the domestic front, shielded from their reactions by refusal to entertain discussion or by actual physical absence. If he ever personally confronted them with an issue, they knew it was something serious.

'Today an inspector from the police came to the surgery,' he said with a small grimace. 'He told me that they'd received an anonymous letter throwing doubt on the circumstances of Grandmother's death. Resentment about her will seemed to be the motivating factor. It's ridiculous, of course, and petty, but I feel that you should all know in case this isn't the end of it.'

Lynn and Deborah had both stopped eating, and stared at him wide-eyed. Only Martin continued shovelling food into his mouth with apparent disregard for the atmosphere.

'We may receive a letter ourselves, or hear gossip that isn't to our liking. I tell you this only to warn you – Martin, your attention, if you please.'

Martin laid down his fork with a clatter and chewed vigorously. 'It's good lamb,' he said, his voice muffled by food. 'No point in letting it get cold.'

Lynn's face wore an anxious frown. 'Who do they think sent this letter?' she asked.

Neville made an impatient gesture. 'The police are not in a position to guess; they don't know our circle of acquaintances.

46

I was shown a portion of the handwriting, but I didn't recognize it.'

'Someone stirring things,' said Martin. 'Trying to create a bit of excitement. I can't say I blame them. This must be the dullest village in the East Midlands.'

'Martin, there's a time to joke and a time to be serious. It's your grandmother whose memory is being besmirched.'

'Martin could be right,' ventured Lynn. 'What exactly was the letter suggesting?'

'That the death was suspicious. As I said, the idea is ridiculous, but I suppose a haemorrhage might sound dramatic to the uninitiated.' He suddenly became aware that Deborah was staring fixedly at her plate and her face was chalk-white. 'We'll say no more about it,' he decreed. 'I just thought you ought to be informed.'

'Silly idea,' said Martin in the kitchen, depositing a trayful of dirty dishes on the draining-board next to Deborah. 'Who'd want to bump the old witch off? She did it herself, in style.'

'Don't,' she said sharply.

'Don't what? Talk about it? Nothing would please dear Father more.'

He sauntered to the door and she swung round, scattering foam from her rubber gloves across the floor.

'Are you going?' she demanded. 'Is that your contribution, one journey from the hatch to the sink?' She answered herself. 'Of course it is. Little boys go out to play, girls stay in and slave away.'

'What's eating you?' he asked. 'I've never washed up.'

'Don't I know it.' She turned back to the sink and began to scrape the congealed remains of dinner off the plates. 'I'll tell you what I can't stand – it's your hypocrisy.'

'This sounds interesting; do continue.'

'You called Grandmother "the old witch" just now, yet you did nothing but suck up to her while she was alive. Mother and I did all the drudging.'

'You were missing the point. The old battleaxe wanted

47

company, someone to tease her a bit, and to listen to stories of how different everything was when she was a girl. It's all there in the Good Book, you know. If you were Martha, then I was Mary – and look who got the gold star.'

'I'm surprised you remember anything from the Bible,' she said, plunging the stack of plates into hot, foamy water. 'You gave up Sunday School when you were ten – and they let you.'

'Poor little Deborah,' he mocked. 'Still has to go to church so that Daddy can keep up appearances. There, there!'

'Oh, just go wherever you were going!'

He danced to the door and paused to deliver the final barb. 'Wrong time of the month, is it?' he asked. 'Never mind, you'll feel better soon.'

Upstairs, Neville was changing his clothes to go out for another evening meeting. He selected a tie from the wardrobe and held it against his shirt to ensure a perfect colour match, then walked towards Lynn who was putting his clean socks away in a drawer.

'I've been thinking about George,' he announced. 'His chest's really bad these days and he can't get about much. That flat of his is up two flights of stairs. While Mother was here, we weren't in a position to give him much help, but now that she's gone I think we should offer him a home. He's family, and we can make sure he's properly taken care of.'

Lynn felt herself go cold. She was aghast at the proposal. Neville's younger brother George was only forty-eight, but a lifetime of immoderate habits and reckless disregard for his health had left him a shell of a man who would easily pass for sixty. In his youth he had gone to sea to assuage severe asthma, but engines fascinated him, and soon he was breathing long days of asbestos and hot diesel fumes, and long nights of cigarette haze. An equal fondness for alcohol and women had led to brushes with more dubious medical conditions than asthma, but now he had been invalided out of the Merchant Navy and lived alone in a squalid little flat near the town centre. Allergies apart, all he had in common with his brother was the shape of their ears.

'He . . . we can't,' she stammered.

'Oh, he won't be a lot of trouble. He doesn't even smoke now; he's trying to safeguard what's left of his lungs. Now we've got the room, people will expect us to show some charity.'

That was the crux; *people would expect*. Lynn felt her teeth clench. Neville's every move was dictated by image, the done thing, conforming to others' conceptions of an exemplary, caring GP. But what about her? For him the gesture was cheap, for her it meant a return to that slavery – yes, slavery – she had endured for eight years with Maud. How could he even think of installing another invalid? And she had always felt uneasy near George, with his yellow teeth and lecherous eyes.

'He won't want to stay here,' she said faintly. 'We're too conservative for him. He values his freedom.'

Neville pulled on a jacket and assessed his appearance briefly in the wardrobe mirror. 'You'll find that George has changed,' he said. 'He's getting tired; he knows he's ill.'

'He'll have some money from Maud soon; he could engage a private nurse.' Lynn's heart thumped wildly as she waited for Neville's response.

'He could, but he likes the idea of coming here.'

'You mean you've already asked him?'

'I've simply floated the notion.'

Lynn found herself so choked with rage and fear that she didn't know where to look. She went to the window and stared down into the garden. At first she saw only a green blur as the power of her emotions impeded the visual signals reaching her brain, but gradually the messages unscrambled and details swung into clarity. How fine the shrub roses were this year! Look at the cascade of honeysuckle embracing the pergola! The lavender had spread out to form a rich mattress . . .

Movement arrested her attention. There, directly below, was Henry trying to stalk a thrush in his clumsy fashion. He crawled across the grass, rear end rolling, tail twitching – but just as he was ready to strike, another bird arrowed overhead and chirruped a raucous warning. As the cat lunged, his

49

intended victim took flight, leaving him alone in the centre of the vast lawn, looking round foolishly, ears flattened in mortification.

Poor Henry . . . He was too fat, too slow, his fur too vivid a ginger to escape detection.

Lynn held her breath. Fur . . . asthma . . . salvation? She turned back to face Neville, who now stood immaculate in his suit. 'It would be too dangerous for George to live with us,' she said. 'Don't you remember? Apart from all the pollens from the garden, he's acutely allergic to cats. Much more than you are.'

'Of course I remember. I've considered that factor. Henry will have to be disciplined, and kept to limited areas of the house. We should have enforced this years ago, for Deborah's sake. It's unhealthy the way he's allowed to shed hairs on sofas and piles of linen; cats can carry all kinds of diseases. No – he must live in the conservatory from now onwards, and the utility room if the weather is particularly cold.' He pushed back a crisp white cuff and consulted his wristwatch. 'I must go now,' he said. 'There's no more time for discussion.'

Lynn didn't follow him downstairs. She felt drained and sick, and sat down cautiously on the bed like someone who wasn't quite sure where her limbs were. Naturally there was no more time to talk. He had broached the subject at a carefully chosen moment, as always, and when next they spoke her assent to his scheme would be taken for granted. Forget the job at the optician's; forget the new hairstyle which Neville hadn't even noticed . . . Defeat, that familiar shade, was back in his place at her shoulder, and she knew her cause was already lost.

Soundlessly she began to cry.

7

'Why haven't you acted? It was probably poison. Maud Witherspoon wasn't all that ill.'

Montgomery stared at the blue sheet in his hand and clucked his annoyance. He had hoped that this little episode had blown over, that one blast of venom from the anonymous letter writer had provided the necessary catharsis. Now here was another missive.

'What do you think, Will?' he asked. 'I suspect our correspondent is unhinged.'

Sergeant Bird took the letter in his large hand. 'I'd agree, sir. From what you told me of the circumstances of the lady's death, it all sounded quite above board. Mind you, if she'd died just *before* attempting to change her will, I'd have looked upon it differently.'

'Well, she didn't. We're left with two malicious letters, and I'm loath to waste resources chasing them up when we've so much else going on. What can we do that's quick and painless?'

'Submit them for graphological analysis.' He grinned. 'That is, if you believe in it.'

Montgomery nodded a rueful concession. 'I admit to ambivalence in that direction,' he said. 'They don't always get the character profiles right. But it would certainly be of value if we had a suspect's handwriting for comparison . . . ' He paused. 'There might just be a way to achieve that.'

*

'Carole . . . ' Montgomery placed his hands on her shoulders as she stood guard over the kitchen cooker.

'You want something.'

'Just a small piece of espionage.'

'One of your cases?' She twisted round to look at him, her face alight.

'I can hardly dignify it with the title "case". We've been receiving mysterious letters at headquarters, and the writer may possibly be someone you've met – a Mrs Weddell Grant.'

'Oh.'

'You're going to a Ladies' Friendship Guild meeting on Wednesday night, aren't you? She's the vice-president, I believe. Is there any chance you could get hold of a sample of her writing?'

Carole's enthusiasm had visibly dimmed. 'Drat,' she said. 'It *would* be the LFG, wouldn't it? Actually, Richard, I'd intended to ring Joan and cry off Wednesday because it really isn't my kind of organization. So far I've been attending as a probationary member, but if I turn up much more they'll expect me to join. Is it important?'

'It might be.'

'The Weddell Grant's an awful woman. She's bossy, obvious and somehow – lacking in class.'

'That could be useful. She sounds the type who'd swallow flattery. Ask her to write down a recipe or something.'

'This will cost you,' warned Carole, 'whether or not I can deliver. You're asking a lot.'

'Name your price.'

'Dinner at the Four Seasons.'

'London? Paris? New York?'

'Nottingham will do.'

'Agreed,' he said.

Thorbeck Village Hall was the LFG's regular venue, being a dry, well-structured stone building of large capacity. Carole was glad of the size as she sat through an earnest demonstration of *cloisonné*, but found herself feeling somewhat claustrophobic at the end when the press of women surged towards the refreshments table.

Joan didn't help. Whenever she went out with Carole, she adopted a schoolgirl 'best-friends' mentality, giggling in her ear, hardly leaving her alone for a second. Carole would need all her powers of concentration if she was to get within ten feet of the Weddell Grant, let alone persuade her to part with a sample of her handwriting.

The chattering all around was collectively numbing, but a few fragments of conversation stood out above the rest:

'. . . such a dreadful place. It ought to be closed down. They say it's like a *drug* . . . '

'She'll be the new treasurer for Hope in the City . . . '

'George is with them now: the black sheep. I don't know how they'll manage. He never did get on with Neville . . . '

Joan nudged her familiarly in the ribs. 'Gossip expands to fit the time available,' she averred, her voice shaking with mirth.

They edged their way forward until they came alongside a table laden with cakes and sandwiches. Here, a woman with grey-streaked dark hair and a thin, sour face turned round to Joan.

'I've been telling them for years,' she grumbled. 'Two tables would be much better. Similar food on each. This way, the tea is always cold when you get to it . . . '

'Who was that?' whispered Carole when the woman had insinuated her crow-like frame near the head of the queue under the guise of speaking to someone else.

'Oh, you needn't bother with *her*. That's Harriet Lawson. Always whingeing about something. She's one of those perpetually dissatisfied people.'

Carole surveyed the fare on offer, and picked out two small sandwiches. The cakes looked uniformly unpromising; she wasn't going to be lumbered with those unless it was in the best of causes. Thinking of which . . .

'Are these all home-made?' she asked in loud, ingenuous tones.

Several ladies gave her their attention. 'Oh yes, duck. It's one of our little rituals.'

'Does everyone bake something? The committee members too?'

''Course they do. Mrs Hoskin makes a lovely chocolate log, and Mrs Weddell Grant does the gingerbread.'

Carole frisbeed a distracted smile in their direction and rapidly scanned the remaining food on the table. Something very dark and nasty-looking, pre-cut in huge hunks, stood in state on a doily-covered white plate in the centre. The ravenous hordes had so far resisted its siren call.

Damn you, Richard, she thought, dropping a leaden portion on to her own plate. She took a cautious nibble. The consistency resembled old mortar; she began to fear for her teeth.

'Is that any good?' Joan again. Well, she was responsible for much of the present situation.

'Try some,' replied Carole.

Ahead, Gertrude Weddell Grant's florid perspiring face suddenly appeared and Carole knew her chance had come. With an action worthy of Harriet Lawson, she slid away from Joan, and seconds later fetched up against Mrs Weddell Grant's fleshy hip.

'Hello, dear. You're our newest recruit, aren't you? I hope you enjoyed the demonstration.'

'Yes . . . fascinating.'

'So glad. We try to ensure that our evenings are of high quality. You'll find the ladies are busy people with fulfilling lives apart from family commitments. What did you say your husband does, dear?'

He's a police officer, and I'm proud of him. 'He's a kind of civil servant. And I work in the library.'

'Ah. Very suitable.'

'Mrs Weddell Grant, I hope you don't mind my saying how – distinctive your gingerbread is. Could I possibly trouble you for the recipe?'

'Certainly.' The woman's glassy blue eyes fixed on a point in the middle distance. 'Sieve together eight ounces of plain flour, three teaspoons of ground ginger, one teaspoon of mixed spice . . . '

'Sorry,' cut in Carole. 'I wonder if you'd write it down for me?'

'I can't, dear. My specs are over there on the committee table. But if you've got a bit of paper, I'll go more slowly. Ready? Eight – ounces – of flour, three – teaspoons – '

Damn you, Richard, thought Carole again as her pen scratched across the back of an envelope. I think tonight has been a waste of time.

'Preliminary report from our handwriting expert,' said Sergeant Bird the following Friday.

'Go on, Will.' Montgomery was on edge. A third anonymous letter had just been opened at the station, giving the lie to his hopes that the matter would simply peter out.

'"The writer is female, right-handed, probably in her forties, and in good physical health. She does, however, suffer from some kind of fixation or source of bitterness."'

'Any delusions? Is she a psychiatric case?'

'There's nothing here to indicate that.'

Montgomery exhaled glumly, looking at the bulging files which covered his desk.

'The timing couldn't be worse,' he said, 'but we're going to have to investigate this properly.'

Trudi Forester was pleasantly surprised by the appearance of the detective inspector her husband had agreed to see at their home. He had an intelligent face with good bone structure, yet the narrow mouth and steely blue eyes hinted at an inner toughness. She glanced at his ring finger; yes – someone had a challenging husband. There were times when her own made her feel short-changed.

'I'm sorry that Ken's out on a call,' she said, 'but he should be back soon.' She led the way into the lounge and motioned Montgomery towards an expensive sofa.

'That's all right. It's good of you both to see me on a Saturday.'

'I understand you're carrying out some enquiries on Neville's behalf.'

'Indirectly. We're investigating allegations which will probably prove to be unfounded, but it would be helpful to us to hear how Dr Witherspoon is regarded by his colleagues.'

She laughed, a social tinkle. 'I think "dull and worthy" would fit the bill.'

'Do patients like him?'

Trudi hesitated. 'Some find him too pompous and don't understand his explanations – all long medical words. They then end up seeing the other partners, even though they remain registered with Neville.'

'Have any patients had a more concrete reason for being disgruntled, do you know? Has Neville ever discussed any unpleasant incidents with you and your husband?'

'No – but then he wouldn't. He's a close type, Victorian, stiff upper lip. He's never shared his family problems with the rest of us.'

'Family problems?'

'Oh,' she shrugged, 'there was a spot of trouble with his boy three years ago. He stole a car and went joy-riding in it. He was charged with reckless driving, but the magistrates gave him a conditional discharge; I imagine that was for his father's sake.'

The detective was watching her intently, and suddenly she sensed that he found her transparent. 'Martin's adopted, you see,' she went on in more indulgent tones. 'I'm sure you get these little hiccups. And Martin probably feels he's asserting his independence by opting for building work as a career.'

'A labourer?'

'Not quite. He's apprenticed to a roofing contractor or whatever they call themselves. Neville would have preferred him to stay on at school.'

'What about the rest of his family?'

'There's nothing much to tell. Both Lynn, his wife, and Deborah, the daughter, are quiet and unremarkable – dour, even. I sometimes think they bring out the stuffier side of Neville's character. It's funny, because he almost married someone quite different . . . '

The front door slammed, and Kenneth Forester hurried in to join them, smoothing the black cap of his hair with one hand.

'Inspector Montgomery – sorry I'm late. I hope my wife has been able to assist you. I had to see a child with croup, and – oh, excuse me.'

In the hall the telephone was ringing. It was a cordless phone, and as the GP stood in the doorway of the lounge, they heard his side of the brief conversation.

'Yes . . . what? When? I see . . . of course; I'll be over straight away.'

'What is it, darling?' Trudi was genuinely concerned; her husband looked perplexed and uneasy as he wandered towards them, still holding the telephone receiver limply in his hand.

'Trouble at Neville's,' he said.

57

8

'I'll stay here this afternoon while you're all out,' said George Witherspoon when lunch was over.

'What, in the dining-room, George?' Neville stopped dabbing at his lip with a napkin and looked at his brother in surprise. 'It's more comfortable in the lounge.'

'I know, but I just fancy sitting near this window with my book. Call it a change of scene.'

'Whatever you like. Have you got your medicines close at hand? Your chest sounds wheezy to me, and you're not very mobile.'

George gave a forbearing yellow smile. 'Neville – I've lived with this demon for years and it hasn't got me yet. The pollens are high, that's all. I heard you sneezing in the bathroom yourself. No, just leave me be and go and enjoy your outing.' He turned to Deborah. 'Are you off to Hardwick Hall with your mother and father?'

Deborah flushed, as she always did when he addressed her directly.

'No,' she said. 'I went there on a school trip two years ago, when we were doing Tudor Studies.'

'But you're going out, aren't you?'

'Yes – to Aileen's.'

'Playing records, I'll be bound, when you should be making the most of this lovely weather.'

'I'm walking there,' she defended herself, and left the room with an awkward smile.

Carefully George rose from his place at table and, using the back of the chair as a support, edged his way to the Parker

Knoll recliner next to the window. Damned fine piece of furniture, this. It supported the small of the back to perfection, tilted at any angle, and even had a built-in footstool. In all his life he had never known luxury like this; Neville had certainly done well for himself.

Gritting his teeth, he lifted his stiff left leg up on to the seat, and installed himself in the chair. It was a nuisance having a gammy leg. He'd broken it in a bar-room brawl in Kowloon, and over the years arthritis had set in: not the type Mother had suffered, thank God, but the doctors didn't want to operate because of his chest . . . George listened to the light wheeze and occasional crackle as he breathed. What did doctors know, anyway? They'd told him he'd grow out of his asthma and here he was, nearly forty-nine and stuck with it.

Creaks sounded from the floor above. Neville had gone upstairs to join Lynn who was getting changed; Deborah, too, was in her bedroom. And Martin –

Careless feet thumped their way down the staircase.

'Psst – Martin,' hissed George as the footsteps passed the dining-room. His nephew appeared, clad in old, frayed jeans and a thin shirt of checked cotton.

'Yeah?'

'Bring me the phone, there's a good lad.'

Martin duly obliged with the cordless telephone from the hall, hung around for a minute, hands in pockets, then drifted out again.

George tapped out a number he had learned by heart, and waited with some trepidation for the reply.

'Evie, girl, is that you? Yes, it's George. Did you get my letter? Yes . . . Do come and see me.' He glanced up as Lynn glided into the room wearing a cream-coloured dress. 'Must go now. Think about it, won't you? 'Bye.' He replaced the receiver with a clatter, discomfited by Lynn's cool eyes.

Nevertheless, she spoke pleasantly enough. 'Have you finished with the phone now, George? Good. I just want to ring Hardwick and check their closing times for the house and garden . . . Thank you.'

He handed it over. 'Nice dress, Lynn.'

She inclined her head; he felt constrained to say more.

'It's good to be with family again,' he fumbled. His chest felt suddenly heavy and tight. 'It's been – too many years away. Now I feel I've served my time; I've come home.'

Her polite smile became fixed. It may have held some warmth, but he couldn't tell; perhaps it was just the closeness of the room.

Lynn made her telephone call in the hall, then waited there for Neville. He had been kind these last two weeks, with little deeds of consideration she knew were his attempts to compensate for George. This trip to Hardwick was a prime example. George himself had mellowed from the lecherous, often foul-mouthed swaggerer she had known before to a maudlin wreck groping for roots and a sense of dynasty. It was the sort of sentiment one usually found in elderly men . . . but then, George was old before his time anyway; it seemed to be a family trait.

I've served my time, he'd said. Yes, he had: his time, his choosing. Now he was trying to integrate, and achieving some success as far as Neville was concerned. Even the children were better behaved in this honeymoon period where everyone strove to please. But when it was over – what then? They would go their ways; she must serve *her* time until death.

Neville pattered down the stairs and picked up his car keys.

'Is everything ready, Lynn?' he asked. 'Henry out?'

'I think so. I saw him in the garden half an hour ago.'

'Let me make sure.' Briskly he walked into the lounge, intending to peer out at the lawn, but as he passed the double doors which led to the adjoining conservatory, he spotted the cat inside among the plants. He was crouched on the tiled floor, lapping water from his saucer.

With a small 'hmm' of satisfaction, Neville checked that the doors were locked and returned to the hall where Martin and Deborah stood chatting with Lynn.

'Do you want a lift to Aileen's?' Neville asked Deborah.

'No thank you. I'm going to walk along the back lane.'

'All right. Your mother and I should be home before six-thirty. We expect to see you by seven at the latest.'

'Yes. Goodbye, Father . . . Mother.'

They each received a light , dry kiss before she opened the front door to leave. Martin followed casually, his crash helmet tucked under one arm.

'Martin?'

'Yes?' Martin turned to face his father, looking bored.

'Where is it that you go every Saturday?'

'Oh – out and about.'

That was as much as he ever told them.

Inside Neville's Granada, Lynn bit her lip with indecision. 'It's very hot, isn't it? It seems to *blast* you as you stand. Perhaps I'd better go and get a hat.'

She noticed his foot begin to tap, but he kept his voice even. 'If we spend our time inside the Hall, you won't need anything on your head.'

'Oh – but now I've thought of it, it'd be silly to leave it behind. Just a moment . . . ' She ducked out of the car and hurried back to the house. Nearly ten minutes passed before she emerged with a wide-brimmed cream sun-hat.

At six o'clock the sun was still high, although the glare of the day had softened. Neville parked the car alongside the house to let Lynn out, then backed it into his double garage.

They entered through the kitchen door, and the air inside was still and heavy.

'I bet George has been napping all afternoon,' said Neville, keeping his voice low to avoid the sound carrying through the flimsy doors of the serving-hatch. 'He'll enjoy a cup of tea. I know I will.'

'We're the first back,' said Lynn, opening the enamel tin

61

where tea-bags were kept. As she went about the business of filling the kettle, Neville wandered through into the hall. He hesitated outside the dining-room door; George was probably asleep even now, or he would have hailed them with some jocular remark. Too much daytime dozing wasn't a good idea, decided Neville. His brother would be coughing and wheezing half the night simply because he was awake. 'We're home, George,' he called, pushing open the door.

The Parker Knoll faced the window; there was no reply from its occupant. Only the edge of George's head was visible, a few crinkled strands of russet hair beyond the beige upholstery of the chair-back. Neville stepped forward. His eyes began to prickle and an irritation teased his nostrils. Allergies! Non-sufferers had no idea how trying a hot summer could be. He skirted round the chair, opening his mouth to speak.

It stayed open. The expression of terror on George's face was like an accusation; even as he lay there dead, the golden cat on his lap uncurled, stretched and blinked up at Neville with lazy amber eyes. Then, obscenely, it started to purr.

Neville found himself clutching at his own collar, his breathing shallow and ragged. All sorts of thoughts stampeded through his brain; he stretched out a hand mechanically to press against George's neck, but the skin was cool and no life pulsed beneath. How could it? That face had set in its dreadful mask hours before and no new wonder-drug from the modern physician's armoury was yet able to create a second Lazarus.

'Neville?'

He looked up. Lynn was in the room, her face uncertain.

'George – is dead,' he said, forcing out the words. Suddenly rage overcame him in a scalding flood. 'I *told* you about this bloody cat!' he yelled. 'You all knew, you all said yes, you'd be responsible. Well, George is dead. Come and look. This bloody cat has killed him!'

He seized her shoulder and propelled her alongside the

body. 'Take a good look. See what happens when we indulge children against our better judgement. Oh – Christ!' He turned his head away as the tickle in his nostrils and throat became intolerable; the sneeze came out more like a sob.

Lynn stood wide-eyed and silent.

He blew his nose. 'Well?' he flayed. 'Well? What have you got to say?'

'I can't believe it. He was fine when we left.'

'Of course he was.'

'What should we do? Ring Dr Quested?'

'No, Kenneth's his GP now.' He took a deep breath, and tried to suppress the trembling in his limbs. 'I'll speak to him. Though he can't do anything except go through the formalities. You take that cat away.' He walked a few steps towards the door, then swung round again. 'He must be put down, Lynn. No arguments. I'll arrange it myself.'

As he stood by the hall telephone, waiting for his partner to answer, Neville watched Lynn carry Henry to the front door, dump him outside and return to the dining-room. Then the connection was made, and he controlled himself enough to outline the situation to Kenneth Forester in a few concise sentences.

Back in the dining-room, Lynn was leaning over the body, apparently extracting something from one of George's trouser pockets.

'What have you got there?' he asked.

She started. 'Nothing . . . I was checking to see if he had an inhaler with him. There doesn't seem to be one within reach. I wondered if – it would have made any difference.'

Neville gave a non-committal shrug. 'Who can say?'

Lynn left the room, murmuring about tea, the fingers of her right hand curled into her palm. He was sure she was carrying something. Quietly he followed, and lurked outside the open kitchen door as she pressed the pedal of the waste-bin with her foot. He saw a flutter of blue.

It was only when Kenneth Forester's car drew up outside that the chance arose to investigate. As Lynn went to the front door, Neville opened the bin. On top of a mound of tin cans, vegetable parings and soggy kitchen roll lay a broken stem. It had leaves the colour of sage. It had tiny purple flowers, like miniature irises.

It was catmint.

Montgomery took careful note of his surroundings as the car turned into Neville Witherspoon's drive. The house, Oaklands, was large, as he had expected: a modern brick detached with picture windows and gables. It was set back from the road, and screened from neighbouring properties by trees. The drive itself curved round to the left of the building to terminate in a triangular parking area; both drive and area were composed entirely of pink bricks in a herringbone pattern, a surface Montgomery knew to be one of the most expensive available – weeks before he had regretfully turned down an estimate to have his own pitted concrete forecourt replaced by something similar. He climbed out of the car; the evening was balmy and peaceful. It was hard to imagine that tragedy had occurred behind these honeysuckle-framed windows.

Neville Witherspoon was not pleased to see him. His words, as Kenneth Forester bustled inside to examine the body, were 'What are you doing here?' He recovered enough, however, to introduce his wife to Montgomery, who received an impression of someone mousy and insignificant.

The three men congregated around George, while Lynn hovered in the background.

'Poor old feller,' said Kenneth as he went about his procedures. 'You say you found him at six? I would estimate that he died between two and three o'clock.' He looked up at Neville. 'I didn't know he'd been deteriorating. I would have come to see him.'

'He hadn't. He had a mild wheeze, as always, but he was coping well with the summer pollens. The salbutamol tablets you prescribed seemed to suit him.'

'Did he take them properly?'

'Yes.'

'I saw him this lunchtime,' said Lynn. 'He took all his tablets with water.'

Kenneth closed his bag with a puzzled frown on his face. 'A sudden, acute asthma attack is possible,' he said, 'but I can't be certain enough to sign a certificate. I'm sorry, Neville, but I think there should be a PM. Just to be on the safe side.'

'You know his history. What else would it have been?' Neville sounded defensive, and cast a venomous look towards Montgomery.

'Cardiac failure, perhaps. I was beginning to wonder about his heart. That's why I switched him away from the aminophylline.'

Neville sighed. 'Actually, Kenneth, we think we know what precipitated his asthma. Deborah's cat had got in here by mistake, and George was very allergic to cat fur.'

'Yes; I know. I did the scratch tests. Are you sure the cat came near him?'

'It was sitting on his knee.'

Kenneth was silent for a moment; he looked shocked.

'So you see we don't need to trouble the coroner,' said Neville. 'You've examined George within the last fourteen days, so it's all straightforward. Thank you for coming, and – ' He broke off as his partner slowly shook his head.

'I'm sorry, Neville. You're probably right about the cause of death, but I'd rather be sure.'

Neville turned away angrily. 'Then people will talk, all over again. Or should I say "go on talking"? I suppose you and Inspector Montgomery were having a cosy little chat about me.'

'I'm afraid it was another letter,' said Montgomery. 'That's the only reason I'm here today.'

'More fuel for the gossips,' muttered Neville bitterly. 'A GP should be above reproach. I've done nothing wrong, yet there are whispers everywhere.'

'An orderly post-mortem will silence them,' soothed Kenneth. 'There'll be no fodder for their tongues once the cause of death is known and understood.'

As the younger doctor spoke, Montgomery leaned over the body and removed a wisp of ginger cat fur from a fold at the front of George Witherspoon's trousers. Then his sharp eyes spotted something else; a tiny purple bell was protruding from the pocket. He picked up the flower head and held it lightly in his left hand while he dug further with the right. This time the haul was a crushed four-inch stem of catmint.

'Does your cat like catmint?' he asked neutrally.

'Oh – yes. He spends all day sleeping in clumps of it. Sometimes he rolls on the stems and picks up bits in his fur. Isn't that so, Lynn?'

'Yes.'

'This piece came from George's pocket – *inside* the pocket.'

'Well . . . I don't know. George hadn't been out for days.' Neville flashed a doubtful glance at Lynn, but her attention seemed to have wandered.

'The mint is fresh,' said Montgomery.

'I think I hear Martin coming,' broke in Lynn. 'One of us must explain what's happening – I'll go.'

Sure enough, a motor bike spluttered to a halt on the bricked area outside. They heard the front door open and, shortly after, murmured voices in the hall.

The three men stood awkwardly around the body.

'Has your son been out all afternoon?' Montgomery asked Neville.

'Yes. He left with Deborah about twenty to two. Lynn and I followed a few minutes later. Poor George had no one to help him. If we'd known, we'd have left a telephone nearby, but the attack must have overpowered him very rapidly.'

'George had a stiff leg,' explained Kenneth Forester. 'He had to hobble to get about the house.'

There was something Montgomery wanted to know from Kenneth, but he felt reticent about asking in front of Neville. Still, police officers were rarely allowed the luxury of good taste.

'That expression of fear,' he said, nodding towards George's gaping mouth and staring eyes, 'is it consistent with death during an asthma attack?'

'Oh, yes,' said the GP calmly. 'Any form of respiratory embarrassment, in fact. In cardiac failure when the lungs fill with fluid the unfortunate patient often looks like this.' He lifted a nearby limb and tested the degree of muscle tone. 'We should lay him out soon, I think. A pillow under the jaw and

the eyes closed . . . May I make the necessary arrangements?'
He addressed them both, and Neville nodded heavily.

By eight-thirty Montgomery was becoming restless. He was
waiting in the lounge for Deborah, and she was not yet home.
The boy Martin had been little help; he had mumbled, dis-
closed nothing useful, and been glad to escape to his room at
the earliest opportunity. Now the Witherspoons were beginning to wonder what was delaying their daughter.

'We said seven o'clock,' said Lynn; it was the fifth time she
had made this observation. 'She's never late.'

'I'll ring Mrs Blanchard. Is her number in the book?' Neville
looked exhausted and unhappy.

'No – I'll go,' said Lynn, and slipped out into the hall.
Within minutes she returned, clearly worried. 'Aileen's
mother has just got back herself, but she's spoken to Aileen,
and Deborah left their house at a quarter to six!'

'Twenty minutes,' murmured Neville. 'Twenty-five if she
dawdled . . . she should have been home just after us.'

'She walked?' probed Montgomery.

Lynn answered him. 'Yes. Her friend Aileen lives on the
Clarkwood Estate, towards town. It's ten minutes away by
bus, but only about twenty on foot because of a short cut the
local people call the "back lane". It starts behind these houses
and tracks through a copse on the side of the hill. Deborah
often uses it at weekends . . . ' Her voice began to wobble, and
she stared distractedly at Neville. 'We must go and look for
her now! Perhaps she's had an accident.'

'In a moment,' he said. 'Let's be scientific about this. She
may have come home and been frightened by all the com-
motion. Let's just see . . . ' He paused as Martin passed the
open door, dressed in his best beige suit. 'Martin! You're not
going out, are you?'

Martin flushed. 'I just thought . . .'

'Your sister isn't home yet. Have you any idea why?'

'Hardly. I don't know what she gets up to with Aileen.'

'She hasn't been in and left again while we were all occupied, has she?'

'I never saw her – but I'll check her room.' Martin thundered up the stairs, but came back more slowly.

'Mother,' he said. 'Could you come and look? Deborah's room doesn't look right; she's been throwing clothes around, and I think her suitcase has gone.'

They all followed him up the stairs to a small bedroom with pink wallpaper. Apart from a few garments strewn across the bed, Montgomery noticed that everything was neat and tidy. There were no posters of pop stars or film heroes on the walls, just a painting of a lion's head and a framed certificate awarded for a school cookery competition. The books on the shelf were all classics.

Lynn pulled on the wardrobe door and riffled frantically through the clothes inside. Then she attacked the chest of drawers, repeating her inspection with trembling hands.

'What was on here?' asked Montgomery quietly, gesturing towards a white-painted dressing-table whose glass top was completely bare.

'N-not very much,' stammered Lynn. 'A brush and comb; talc, a roll-on . . . Neville . . . ' Her eyes filled with tears. 'She's gone! She's taken her things, and gone.'

'My daughter would have left a note.'

'There isn't one – unless it's downstairs.'

Martin stood in the doorway, distancing himself from the emotion. 'She can't have left home,' he said. 'She's too fond of Henry.'

'Henry!' Lynn shot a look of accusation at her husband before hurrying downstairs and disappearing into the lounge. Montgomery, who had yet to meet this cat, kept up as best he could. He found Lynn unlocking the double-glazed doors which led to the conservatory; together they stepped through into its semi-tropical ambience. The air was heavy with green and woody scents, and attractive rattan furniture stood between plant-holders on the quarry-tiled floor. Dusk was approaching, but one pane of glass gleamed furnace-gold in a final salute from the westering sun.

'His carrying basket has gone,' said Lynn. Her voice sounded flat, defeated.

'Is this where Henry normally lives?' asked Montgomery as the others joined them with sober faces.

'Since George came,' said Lynn, 'we confined Henry to the conservatory here. He could get in and out through the cat-flap – ' she pointed to the outer door, 'and sleep on this padded chair. We've always kept the carrying basket near to Henry's sleeping area, so that he'd become familiar with it and not make a fuss if we had to use it to take him to the vet.'

'If Deborah has taken the cat, how do you think she did it? You've only just unlocked the doors from the lounge.'

Lynn didn't hesitate. 'We keep the outer conservatory door unlocked until last thing,' she said. 'She'll have come in from the garden.' Her eyes went back to Neville with the same hostile glint Montgomery had noticed in the bedroom. 'You realize what's happened, don't you,' she said. 'Deborah must have come home just after us. She heard you through the hatch – everything you said about putting Henry down. That's why she's gone. You've driven our daughter away!'

Montgomery stood in the lounge, taking a quiet moment for thought before the inevitable plunge into administrative activity. Lynn was on the telephone, speaking to a former neighbour, while Neville and Martin milled about aimlessly.

An unhappy household and an altered will; anonymous letters . . . a suspicious death . . . another suspicious death, and a missing schoolgirl . . . All this was a fine cat's-cradle of innuendo, but no solid evidence of a crime had emerged. Only one course of action would clear the mists, and it would be about as welcome to Neville as a fly in one of his sterile dressings packs. Montgomery sighed. Maud Witherspoon would have to wait a little longer for her final rest; he was going to seek an exhumation order.

9

The residents of Thorbeck awoke on Tuesday to a delightful treat. Not since Noah Farnborough's pacemaker had exploded in the crematorium had there been a scandal of such quality. Screens surrounded Maud Witherspoon's hillside grave below St Michael's, and the word was that 'they' had dug her up at dawn and transported the body to the Victoria Hospital.

Harriet Lawson tapped her way along the village's main street, looking for people who had yet to hear the news. Her gait was distinctively short-stepped (once described by Martin Witherspoon as 'like a chicken in leg-irons'); anyone who fell into her company was thus forced to stay with her for longer than they would have chosen. Today, Gertrude Weddell Grant rolled out of the post office just as Harriet was passing.

'Gertrude, good morning. Have you heard the news?'

'About Deborah Witherspoon? The poor child's still missing. It's been two full days now.'

'No. I meant Maud.'

'What about Maud?'

'They – *disturbed her rest* a few hours ago.' Harriet pursed her lips in a pious expression, but her eyes glittered. 'It's quite shocking. Tragic for the family, of course.'

The larger woman looked dazed. 'You mean she's been *exhumed*?' she stammered.

Harriet nodded, and her voice was hushed. 'Yes.'

'But what do they hope to find?'

'Who can say? They must have suspicions of some nature; she did die suddenly.' She shot a crafty glance at Gertrude's

70

uneasy face. 'If I were you, I wouldn't count on that legacy for Hope in the City for a while. This is bound to delay the distribution of the estate.'

Gertrude peered up the street as if seeking an escape. 'You obviously haven't heard *all* the news, Harriet. The charity won't be receiving a penny. The will was invalid.'

'Oh, I *am* sorry.'

'I'm sure. But this other business – tsk! One can only feel sorry for the Witherspoons.'

And even sorrier for oneself, thought Harriet.

In the Venning Road surgery, Neville sat slumped at his desk with a pile of patients' record cards in front of him. He knew that work was the only way to keep the day's unpleasantness at bay, and fortunately for him there was plenty of it. It was different for Lynn at home ... no, he wouldn't think of that. Neither would he dwell on the niggling question which he dared not ask her. Resolutely he picked up the first card.

'Neville?'

He lifted his head at the sound of Katherine Adams's dark chocolate voice. She glided into the room, tall and graceful, and halted by his chair.

'I'm so sorry about Deborah,' she said. 'Is there any news?'

'No.'

'Tell me what I can do to help. I can scour any area with the car, day or night, or make telephone calls. Just say what is needed.'

'Thank you, Katherine. I will.'

Her hand touched his shoulder for a moment, and he smelt the subtle cologne on her wrist. It reminded him of an occasion years before.

'Katherine,' he said as she started to walk away. He felt vulnerable, a supplicant. It was a situation of which he had little experience.

Her brown eyes regarded him steadily.

'Do you ever find yourself wishing you could turn the clock back?' he asked.

'No,' she said. 'Not now, not for a long time.'

The post-mortem was over. Montgomery waited by the sluice room adjoining the mortuary, and tried without success to banish the smell of death from his nostrils. The mortuary assistant, a little goblin of a man, made things easier: this was so obviously just everyday work to him. His casual comments made the attainment of a similarly nonchalant demeanour a matter for personal pride.

Montgomery had the experience to cope. Sergeant Bird, as the most phlegmatic of all his colleagues, would have been the ideal companion but he was otherwise engaged, so Detective Constable Graham Smythe had been given an opportunity to experience something new. It now looked as if that young man would be on sick leave for the rest of the day.

Frobisher, Nottingham's Home Office pathologist, rustled across to join him, having finished his dictation and instructions for the various specimens.

'It's interesting,' he said, turning the taps on full. 'The gastric erosions I demonstrated could certainly have caused the fatal haemorrhage, but that still leaves us with unexplained minor bleeding at other sites in the body. Those would seem to indicate the presence of a haemorrhagic diathesis.'

'I beg your pardon?'

'Inadequate coagulation – something making the blood too thin. It might simply have been a coexistent medical problem, but she may equally have had something administered to bring this about. I can't give you a definitive answer without specific tests.'

Montgomery felt a stir of excitement; here was at least a hint of vindication for the time he had so far spent on the case. 'Ask them to rush the tests through, if they can,' he said. He and Frobisher had known each other for many years. 'What about George Witherspoon?' he went on. 'I gather you did his PM, too.'

'Yes. He seemed to have neglected himself a bit; there were

changes in the liver consistent with longstanding alcohol abuse, but the actual cause of death did appear to have been an acute attack of bronchial asthma. I could find no other pathology.'

'Were you able to estimate the time of death?'

'He died no later than two hours from the start of his last meal.'

'Thank you.'

Montgomery left the mortuary without too much haste, and drove back to the station to find that William Bird had returned from his own enquiries. Together they went to Montgomery's office.

'How was the PM?' asked Sergeant Bird.

Montgomery smiled thinly. 'Smythe is still recovering. Apropos of Maud Witherspoon, though, there are hopeful signs: Frobisher says she did die because of bleeding from gastric erosions, but he thought her blood clotting may have been abnormal. That could have been drug-induced. We won't know for sure until Toxicology reports on the samples.'

'What about George?'

'Acute asthma attack.'

'So there was nothing actually criminal about his death?'

'No – but plenty one could describe as abnormal. The family knew that cats affected George severely, yet one still ended up trapped in a room with him. And that's the day the daughter went missing.'

Sergeant Bird raised his eyebrows. 'Would you give me a rundown on the situation, sir? I've finished with the Reckman case now, so I could be of some help.'

'Gladly. The Witherspoons live in a very attractive detached house at Thorbeck. Neville, the father, is a GP; his wife Lynn looks after the home, and their two children still live there. Martin is eighteen and adopted; he seems to be a bit of a rebel and works for a roofing contractor. Deborah, their natural child, is a schoolgirl of fifteen.

'When Maud, the grandmother, died, they had a spare room to offer Neville's brother George, a single man who had been living in relative poverty these last few years. Before retiring early due to his bad chest, George had been a merchant seaman – an engine-room rating, in fact. When he came to Thorbeck, the family made special arrangements for Deborah's cat Henry, to make sure that George was never exposed to the fur. Henry lived in the conservatory, with free access to the garden via a cat-flap.

'On Saturday, the family had an early lunch because Neville and Lynn Witherspoon were going to Hardwick Hall – that's a favourite haunt of yours, isn't it?'

'One of the finest examples of Elizabethan architecture in the country,' supplied Sergeant Bird, who was drawn to all things historical. 'We're well blessed in this region.'

'True. Anyway, lunch was over by one-fifteen, and George was seen to take his pills in the proper manner. At about one-forty Martin and Deborah left, then shortly before two the parents went off on their trip, leaving George locked in the house. He had chosen to stay in the dining-room – he had a gammy leg and couldn't move very quickly. Henry had been checked, and was out in the conservatory.

'The parents were the first to return, at six o'clock, and they discovered the body almost immediately. George was where they had left him, still seated in the dining-room, but now the cat was on his lap, purring. When I saw him myself half an hour later, he looked long gone, and I have it from Frobisher that he must have died within two hours of starting his last meal – which means that he was dead by three. A sprig of catmint was in his trouser pocket; no one could provide a sensible explanation for that.

'Naturally, there was a lot of tension and activity once the discovery had been made, so it wasn't realized at first that Deborah was late home. Martin had arrived on his Suzuki at a quarter to seven, but it was eight-thirty before anyone started looking for Deborah in earnest. We found that she had sneaked in without anyone noticing, and left again with a suitcase of clothes, and the cat in a wicker basket.'

'May I just interrupt?' asked Sergeant Bird. 'What if either Martin or Deborah had come home early and wanted to gain access? Was George supposed to open the door?'

'No; he was scarcely mobile. I understand that Martin has

his own key, and another is kept in a secret place by the garage for use in emergencies.'

'What about telephones? Was there one within George's reach?'

Montgomery shook his head. 'The nearest was in the hall. Another is situated in Neville's study.'

'I see. Do go on.'

'The general feeling was that Deborah had come in just after her parents, and heard them talking through the thin doors of the serving-hatch. Neville was angry and upset, and threatening to have Henry put down. She must have regarded that as a very real danger. We think she hid in the utility room while he rang for Dr Forester and Lynn made tea. She probably only came out when Forester and I arrived and everyone was in the dining-room again. She crept upstairs, packed a bag, left by the kitchen door again and went round the outside of the house to find Henry.

'Lynn had thrown him out of the front door, and I imagine he had wandered back to the conservatory where his food and water bowls were. Wherever he was, Deborah found him, shut him in the carrying basket and left the premises without a word.'

'Not even a scribbled note, or phone call?'

'Nothing.' Montgomery took a deep breath. 'You'd think it would be easy, wouldn't you, tracing a young girl who left a village carrying a suitcase and a basket with a large ginger cat inside it. But no one has seen her. She could just about have struggled back to her friend Aileen along a quiet lane, but Aileen's mother assured us that Deborah wasn't there. Deborah has few friends, and her other possible destination, a former neighbour she used to confide in, has proved a blank. She's simply vanished.'

'Money?'

'She had some cash in a money-box, perhaps as much as forty pounds, and a building society pass book.'

'Do you think she had a boyfriend with a car?'

'It's very unlikely. Everything that I gleaned from her family seemed to point to Deborah's being childlike and naïve. She was shy, studious and rather prickly. Her bedroom reflected old-fashioned tastes.'

'She took a taxi, then. Is there a phone box in the village?'

'Yes – but bad news. We did work that one out for ourselves, and officers enquired from every firm about a young girl with any kind of luggage being picked up in Thorbeck – without result. We showed her photograph as well: this one.' Montgomery opened the front of a slender file and turned it round for Sergeant Bird to see: it was an official school portrait of Deborah Witherspoon.

'With the right make-up she could look older,' mused Sergeant Bird.

'I agree, but she wasn't allowed to use any at home. I suspect that Neville wanted to keep her a little girl as long as possible.'

'Hmm. What now?'

'We continue enquiries into the disappearance. The cat is surely her biggest liability, so I've got Jackson checking every cattery and animal charity in the district, in case Deborah has sought temporary boarding for Henry. The best thing you and I can do is get an accurate picture of the family background, because if we know what makes Deborah tick, we're half way to finding her.'

He looked at his watch. 'Aileen will be at school, so I suggest we try the family friend who lives in Mapperley – Mrs Angela Cording.'

Angela Cording was a tall, bony woman whom Montgomery judged to be in her mid-forties. Her detached house stood in the middle of a row of similar properties and its interior bore witness to work done at home.

'I write articles for a local magazine,' she smiled. 'Please ignore these papers. Do sit down.'

A tortoiseshell cat lifted a sleepy head as Sergeant Bird deposited himself next to it on the settee; he offered it a few encouraging clucking noises and fondled the silken ears.

'That's Minou,' said Mrs Cording. 'She's eleven now. Deborah was very fond of her ... You said on the telephone you wanted to ask me something about Deborah?'

76

'Yes,' said Montgomery. 'I believe Mrs Witherspoon rang you on the night she first went missing...'

Angela Cording stared at him, her eyes suddenly distressed. 'You mean she's still missing? Oh, my goodness. That's dreadful. I had no idea. Poor Lynn.'

'We felt if we spoke to someone who knew the family well, it would give us the best chance of working out where Deborah might have gone to. How long have you known the Witherspoons?'

'Let me see ... They moved in next door – the Sandtexed house – about nine years ago. Yes: Martin was nine, and Deborah six. A year later, Neville's mother Maud came to join them after selling her own house. She was troubled by arthritis and needed some care. Perhaps you know that she died recently?'

Montgomery nodded. 'Were they a happy family?'

'Well – not exactly. At least, I didn't think so. Lynn used to come round for coffee sometimes, and although she tried to be loyal, I could tell she found Maud a trial. Neville had been engaged to someone else, you see, and broken it off to marry Lynn instead; Maud was constantly letting it be known that she thought he'd made a mistake. Lynn felt both resentful and insecure.'

'At least Neville had chosen her to marry.'

'Yes – but it seems it was for a purpose. His former fiancée had been a professional woman who wasn't interested in having children early. Neville, in his late twenties, had decided that the best image for a caring family doctor was a man with his own wife and family; in fairness, I'm sure he wanted the patients to feel that he could empathize fully with their problems. So he married Lynn, who was only nineteen, with the intention of starting a family straight away.

'Of course, these things don't always work out according to plan. I gather he approached the whole issue like a military campaign, and blamed Lynn when he was thwarted. After years of trying, she became terribly depressed, and they adopted Martin.'

'A joint decision, presumably.'

Mrs Cording hesitated, and glanced at Montgomery's face

as if assessing his integrity. 'I . . . listen, Inspector, please don't tell Lynn I said this, but – she never wanted to adopt. She wanted her own baby, and knew it was only a matter of time. Neville forced his will on her, and she was unable to stand up for herself.'

She looked down at her hands. 'For the first few years, I believe she actually hated Martin, and she spoiled him badly out of guilt. Both parents did. Then, when Deborah came along, they realized what a little terror they had created, and determined not to repeat the misjudgement. Poor Deborah has always received the strictest discipline; she used to call round here in tears, saying how unfair it was, how Martin was allowed so much more leeway than she. But the truth was, they'd given up with him.'

'How would you describe Deborah's character?'

'It's very much like her mother's. She can be really sweet and generous towards people she likes – loyal, too. But she is introverted, and sometimes mulish.'

'Does she have a temper?'

'Oh yes. I remember she would occasionally hit out if she thought it was in a good cause.'

'And Lynn?'

Angela Cording looked thoughtful, and a little disturbed. 'Lynn is one of those people who suppresses anger and lets it build up inside her. I think marriage to Neville has done that. When she does let fly, it's quite disproportionate, and a total shock to whoever caused the problem. Me, I tell people early if they're getting up my nose, then they have fair warning.'

'Who were Deborah's friends, Mrs Cording?'

'I don't know. She must have had some friends at school, but she never brought anyone back for tea. Peter and I have no children, so she had no immediate neighbours to play with . . . but she loved Minou. It's because of Minou that she pestered her parents to buy her a kitten, and eventually they allowed her to keep Henry.'

'I saw a clump of catmint in your garden,' said Montgomery conversationally. 'Are all cats attracted to it?'

Angela Cording smiled. 'It's funny – I planted that years ago for Minou, and she remains supremely indifferent. Yet the cats across the road go crazy for it; they roll on the clump and end up in a kind of psychedelic ecstasy, as if they'd taken LSD.'

'Did Henry like the smell?' asked Sergeant Bird, trying not to chuckle as Minou licked the back of his hand with her rough little tongue.

'Oh, he did! The children used to tie a bunch to the end of a piece of string, and run round the garden; he'd follow it anywhere.'

'Do you see much of them now?' enquired Montgomery.

The amusement in Angela Cording's face was lost to regret.

'Very little,' she said. 'They left three years ago, and apart from Christmas cards I've had no contact with the children at all. I've met Lynn twice in town, but only by chance. She doesn't have a car, so it's not surprising and I can't go to Thorbeck because I haven't been invited.' She shrugged. 'It's one of those things.'

'Why did they leave this area? Was it just to buy a bigger house?'

'Partly, but I think it was mainly embarrassment. Martin stole a neighbour's car one night and went roaring round the town, causing considerable damage. Neville tried to compensate the individuals concerned, but the case still got to the juvenile court. Everyone here was talking about it for weeks; the family must have felt that they had to get away.'

'Why do you think Martin took the car?'

'This is only my opinion; I could be wrong . . . I think he was desperate to be noticed.'

The detectives prepared to make their exit, and Angela accompanied them into the hall with an appeal of her own.

'Please do all you can to find Deborah,' she said. 'She must be so mixed-up and alone. And when you do find her – give her my love.'

'School will be out by now,' said Montgomery. 'Let's see what Aileen Blanchard can tell us.'

Twenty minutes later they were inside the modest semi-

79

detached house on the Clarkwood Estate. Sounds from a distant hammer-drill whined through the single glazing, and closer to hand they could hear the lilting patter of a radio disc jockey. Mrs Blanchard, a blonde-haired woman with rather flashy good looks, called up the stairs to Aileen.

'She's just come home,' she explained, 'but we don't want to waste your time; a constable did come and speak to us yesterday.'

'That was routine,' said Montgomery. 'We're trying to fathom why Deborah should run away from home.'

'I can't say I'm surprised,' affirmed Mrs Blanchard. 'I've seen some repressed kids in my time, but Deborah took the cake. We were glad to be able to cheer her up a bit here. Aileen – where *is* the girl? *Aileen! We're waiting for you*! What was I saying? Oh, yes. Deborah had nothing at home but expectations from her parents that she couldn't fulfil.'

Upstairs a door banged, and a light regular tread heralded Aileen's arrival. She was a thin girl with curly blonde-streaked hair and a tip-tilted nose. She wore a tight yellow jumper and dangly enamelled earrings the shape of pineapples.

'Sorry,' she said. 'I was just changing. I hate school uniform.'

'These policemen have come to talk to you about Deborah,' said her mother.

'I don't know anything. I said so before.'

'She was here on Saturday, I understand,' said Montgomery.

'Yes. All afternoon.'

'What did you do?'

'We played records in my room, and we watched a video.'

'They had the place to themselves,' said Mrs Blanchard. 'My husband was putting in some overtime at work, and I was visiting my sister. I came back just after eight o'clock.'

'What was Deborah's manner like while she was here?' Montgomery asked Aileen. 'Was she sad or depressed?'

'No. We were having fun.'

'What time did she leave?'

'Twenty to six.'

'Did she come back again for any reason?'

'That would have been stupid if she was planning to run away; she knew Mum was on her way home.'

A subtle evasion? wondered Montgomery. If Aileen were not an accomplished liar, then here was the perfect place for a direct question.

He looked her straight in the face. 'Aileen – do you know where Deborah is?'

'No.'

Her mother stepped forward urgently. 'Lovey, if you know anything that will help, you must tell us. A girl like Deborah shouldn't be on her own out there. She might come to some harm.'

'I *don't* know where she is – cross my heart and hope to die.'

'Fair enough,' said Montgomery. 'Did she perhaps leave anything here with you – something to collect later?'

'No.' There was insolence in her eyes. 'Have a look if you like.'

'Yes, do,' said her mother, looking at Aileen doubtfully. 'I'd feel happier if you did. The house isn't very big; I'll show you upstairs.'

They all trooped up to the landing, and she paused beneath the attic trap-door. 'Let's start here,' she proposed, and prodded it open with a long-handled hook. She then pulled the steel ladder down, and invited Montgomery to ascend. 'There's a light-switch just ahead,' she added as he vanished into the gloom, 'one of those cords.'

He found it, tugged, and the attic flooded with light; immediately he knew that this room hadn't been disturbed for a long time. The boxes, clothes and general paraphernalia were covered by a fine film of dust, and their neglected air was enhanced rather than reduced by resonant drips and gurgles from the hot water system. He ran his finger along the nearest exposed joist; it came away dirty. Whatever he had hoped to find – Henry, perhaps? – wasn't here.

The next port of call was Aileen's bedroom, a typical teenager's den. Aileen defiantly opened cupboards and drawers, and it was soon clear that nothing of Deborah's could be hidden there.

'I don't know where she is,' she repeated as they cursorily

81

inspected the rest of the house, 'but I don't blame her for going.'

'Why?' asked Sergeant Bird quietly.

'Because her dad doesn't want her to be normal. He wants her to stay at home and have no fun and study sciences, but she doesn't like them and she's no good at them.'

'Has he told her that?'

'He doesn't need to. He buys her chemistry sets and microscopes for her birthdays, and – '

A *clink-clack* sound interrupted her spiel, and moments later Sergeant Bird felt something brush sinuously past his chunky calf. He looked down, and a cross-eyed Siamese cat stared back in his general direction.

'You're favoured,' said Aileen. 'She likes you, so she's making you her property. Her name is Donna. I've got another cat, too. Guess what she's called?'

'Er – Blitzen?' hazarded Sergeant Bird.

Aileen gave a silvery peal of laughter. 'No – it's Bella. *Belladonna*: beautiful lady – and deadly nightshade. Sometimes the pupils of their eyes are enormous.'

'Do you know anyone who's ever looked after Henry for Deborah?'

'No, sorry. Do you want to see outside? I'll show you my guinea-pig.'

Aileen opened the back door and led the way down a short, straight concrete path to a hutch where a rotund specimen with prolific rosettes was eating a carrot. Beside the cage lay a black Dalmatian, gently panting in the heat.

'This is Dandy.' Aileen pointed to the guinea-pig. 'He looks just like a dandelion clock. And that's Austin. Dad chose the name; he said it made a change from Rover.'

The garden was not well cared for. Apart from a haphazard straggle of raspberry canes down one side, it was much as the builders must have left it ten years before: bare, with random patches of rubble and scrubby grass. A new shed, however, stood among the nettles by the lower fence.

'Dad put that up last autumn,' said Aileen. 'He's got some tools and we're going to make a proper garden.'

'May I look?' asked Sergeant Bird.

She shrugged. 'If you want.'

There was no lock on the door, just a hasp. Inside there were indeed tools, and the floor appeared clean, although a faint smell of cat-spray came from somewhere nearby. As Sergeant Bird left the shed, a lean ivory-coloured shape slithered out from the cool shade beneath and stared at him with haughty blue eyes.

'Hello, Bella,' he said.

While Aileen and his sergeant were occupied in the garden, Montgomery turned to Mrs Blanchard.

'Do you know if it's true,' he asked, 'about making Deborah choose science subjects at school?'

'There was certainly pressure from *somewhere*,' she replied. 'I spoke with Deborah once about the GCSEs she would be taking; she didn't sound at all enthusiastic. I enquired about Martin's school career, hoping to draw her out, and her answer was revealing. She said that Martin was the clever one, and he should be studying to be a doctor, not her. From that I concluded that her dad was wanting at least one of the children to follow in his footsteps.'

'I heard that Martin works on a building site.'

'That's right. He gave up his education at the first opportunity, so the onus has fallen on Deborah.'

As Montgomery continued to probe for details of Deborah's life and attitudes, Aileen returned from the garden with Sergeant Bird. Behind her, Austin began a frantic barking.

'What's the matter with that dog?' asked Mrs Blanchard crossly.

Aileen peered through the open doorway. 'It's probably those kids again, the ones from number eleven. They like to get him going; I think they throw things.'

'Well, we don't want another rumpus like Saturday night.' She gave Montgomery an apologetic smile. 'I'm sorry, Inspector. All neighbourhoods have their problems. Is there anything else we can do for you?'

'Yes; try to remember conversations you've had with

Deborah in the past which might yield clues as to her present whereabouts – or Henry's. If an idea strikes you, don't hesitate to ring me at the station. She must be found.'

10

'It was warfarin poisoning,' Montgomery told his assembled detectives. 'Maud Witherspoon was given an anticoagulant, and she bled to death.'

There was a murmur of interest and surprise; Graham Smythe, now recovered from his ordeal, was quick to propound a question.

'Was it rat poison, sir?'

'Certainly not. To kill someone with rodenticide bait, you'd need to administer such huge quantities that your victim would have more than an inkling that something was amiss. No – this warfarin will have come in the handy form of tablets.'

'Could she have been taking them for therapeutic reasons?' Sergeant Bird was ever-cautious.

'I got a list of her drugs telephoned from the surgery; warfarin wasn't one of them. Besides, Dr Quested was treating Mrs Witherspoon for suspected gastric complications, so agents to thin the blood would have been contra-indicated.'

'Murder,' pronounced Brian Jackson, the detective sergeant who usually partnered Smythe.

'Yes. One for sure, possibly two. I've got you all here together so we can consider the circumstances of Maud Witherspoon's death, and look for any motive or opportunity which might implicate an individual, especially if there is a link with George Witherspoon.

'All we know so far is that Maud had lived with Neville and his family for eight years, and latterly had become incapacitated with rheumatoid arthritis. Her friends had to come to her; they were mainly ladies of her own age, or members of the Ladies' Friendship Guild which she had been associated with for decades. This particular organization is independent of churches and the like, but "adopts" charities and raises funds for them. The LFG's vice-president, Mrs Gertrude Weddell Grant, is the treasurer of Hope in the City, a body providing help and advice for youngsters living rough. I gather she's a tireless campaigner.

'The day before she died, Maud Witherspoon elected to change her will. Instead of leaving half of her money to George, and half to the grandchildren Martin and Deborah, she tried to bequeath it all to Hope in the City. She altered her own copy of the original will in the presence of three witnesses, but for technical reasons this proved to be invalid. Her solicitor, Mr Barton, had not been informed; he finds the whole scenario surprising. Everyone agrees she was *compos mentis* at the time, and the theory has been mooted that she was playing some sort of game. We are in no position to make that assumption, but if it *is* true, it throws an interesting side-light on the old lady's character.'

'When did people first know about the change in the will?' asked Jackson.

'A rumour was going round the village at least a week before, and it filtered through to the family. They were too polite to ask her outright.'

'The important thing is if they believed it,' said William Bird. 'It would give them a red-hot motive.'

'Yes, but why kill her *after* the will had been changed? That's what I can't fathom. And if they didn't believe it, why kill her at all? There's another factor to consider, too: who sent the anonymous letters linking her death to the money? Was a troublemaker simply guessing, because of the time factor? Or does somebody *know* something, in which case we must make every effort to track them down?

'We need to answer a number of questions: who visited Maud Witherspoon in the days leading up to her death? Who routinely gave her food and tablets? What was the source of the warfarin? In parallel with this we must look into the circumstances of George Witherspoon's death, the timing of which is highly suspicious. Did *he* know or suspect something? Was he killed for his money? Asthma may be a natural cause of death, but someone let that cat into the dining-room . . .

'And of course there's Deborah,' he went on. 'Our colleagues in the uniformed branch are assisting with the search, but it's up to us to find the leads, the clues to where she's gone. Her money must be running out by now. She's lumbered with an enormous cat. I can't imagine she can stay hidden much longer. So let's be bright, and let's be vigilant. If we find Henry, we find Deborah.'

Montgomery allocated tasks to his small squad of detectives, then returned to his own office to make a telephone call. When he emerged, William Bird caught his attention:

'Are you going to see the Witherspoons?'

'Yes. I've asked that Martin should be present; I want to observe all their reactions first-hand.'

'Mind if I come along?'

'Please do.'

It was lunchtime when they reached Dr Witherspoon's gabled house, and saw that the red Suzuki bike was parked outside. Sure enough, Martin was with his parents as the two officers were shown into the lounge.

'Something about Mother, you said?' was Neville's opening gambit.

'Yes. The post-mortem confirmed a gastric haemorrhage, as you know, but subsequent laboratory tests have shown that there was a reason for this.'

Neville stiffened. 'Wh-what do you mean, "reason"? The "reason" was the state of her stomach. You don't need lab tests to demonstrate that!'

'I'm sorry, Dr Witherspoon. We have proof that she was given warfarin before she died.'

'My God . . . ' Neville Witherspoon's hand went to his mouth; he looked appalled. Montgomery switched his gaze to

87

Martin and Lynn; they wore identical expressions – anxious and wary.

For several seconds no one spoke, then Neville began to bluster. 'We – we always double-check the tablets in the dispensary. I can't understand it . . . she *can't* have been given warfarin. Are you sure?'

'Certain.'

'It's a terrible mistake. I still don't see how . . . ' His voice trailed off miserably.

'We aren't actually treating it as a mistake.'

Having delivered this Exocet, Montgomery stood silent, inviting further contributions. Lynn's face was now completely blank; Martin seemed to be wrestling with some inner conflict. He darted assessing glances at both his parents, then edged towards the bulk of Sergeant Bird at the door and whispered something in his ear. The reply was a monosyllable. Martin swallowed, looked towards his parents again and took two awkward steps forward.

'I did it,' he said. The words were husky; he coughed. 'It was me,' he continued clearly.

'Martin!'

'I'm sorry, Father, but I don't want the wrong people to be blamed. It had to be done; Mother will agree even if you don't.'

'This is ridiculous! Inspector, I don't know why Martin is saying this, but it's sheer nonsense. He couldn't possibly have done any such thing.'

'Please, Inspector, I can't talk here.' Martin looked unhappy and out of place in his dust-streaked building-site apparel. 'I'll tell you everything, but somewhere else.'

Neville advanced furiously, but Montgomery checked him with one flash of his blue-grey eyes.

'We'll sort this out at the station,' he said. 'Is there anything you'd like to bring, Martin?'

The boy shook his head, and they walked out to the car. As Sergeant Bird started the engine, watched intently by Neville through the dining-room window, Montgomery reflected on a piece of notable behaviour he had just witnessed: even as her son was being taken away for questioning, Lynn Witherspoon had neither moved nor uttered a word.

'What did he say to you, Will?' asked Montgomery in a low voice as they prepared to join Martin in the Interview Room.

'He said: "Is he good?"'

'Is who good?'

'You. I said yes.'

'What did you make of it?'

'Presumably he thought that if you were going to ferret out the facts anyway, he might as well tell you, and get some credit for doing so.'

'Hmm. That's one view, for sure . . . Let's hear his story and see if that stands up.'

'I did it,' repeated Martin when the preliminaries were over.

'What did you do?' asked Montgomery.

'I poisoned Grandmother with warfarin tablets.'

'Tell us how and when.'

'I ground them into powder and put them in her tea on Friday morning.'

'Where did you obtain the warfarin?'

'Down at the surgery. There's an unlocked cupboard in Father's office full of free samples from drug reps. I took a packet away with me last time I visited.'

'How did you know how to use this particular drug?'

'Books on medicine and pharmacology. There's a whole row in Father's study at home.'

'Why did you do it?'

Martin hesitated, and absently fingered a scar above his left eyebrow.

'I don't know,' he said.

'You'll have to do better than that. Did you intend that your grandmother should die?'

'Yes.'

'Why?'

Martin cleared his throat, and they saw his shoulders tense. 'Because she was killing Mother,' he said very quietly.

'Speak up.'

'Because she was killing Mother, making her old and grey and depressed. Grandmother had had a good innings, but she was driving everyone else into the ground.'

'I see. Did you take the will into consideration?'

For the first time, a smile appeared on Martin's face. 'Oh, that! Everyone's been making such a fuss, and she was only stringing them along.'

'Is that a guess, Martin?'

'No – she told me, but she swore me to secrecy. It was a bit of fun at the expense of Mrs Waddle Grant or whatever she's called.'

'So the timing of her death was unrelated to the will?'

'From my point of view, yes.'

'But someone wrote letters.'

'Yes.'

'Have you any idea who?'

'Some cat from the Guild, I should imagine. Someone without enough activities to occupy their day.'

'Speaking of cats, what is your opinion of the death of your Uncle George?'

Martin took a deep breath, and they noticed the light tremor of his hands clasped on the desk in front of him. 'I did that as well.'

'Did what?'

'Caused his death – killed him.'

Montgomery raised his eyebrows.

'I did! I went out last Saturday, saw a friend, then came back to the house where Uncle was asleep. I knew he had bad asthma, so I picked up Henry and let him into the dining-room. He's a friendly cat, so I knew he'd look for a lap – and even if Uncle fought him off, enough fur would fly around to start him wheezing.'

'You intended to kill him?'

'Yes.'

'Why?'

90

'Same reason as before. It was no good removing Grandmother from the scene if another invalid was going to install himself and keep Mother just as trapped.'

'Where did you get that scar from, Martin?'

Martin looked puzzled for a moment. 'Oh – it's nothing. You always get a bit of rough-and-tumble within families.'

'Did your father hit you?'

'God, no! He's far too uptight for that, and I'm his size now, anyway.'

'Deborah?'

'Look – it doesn't matter. It doesn't bother me.'

'All right. Tell me the name of this friend you visited on Saturday.'

'Ray Cooper.'

'Is Ray a builder?'

'Well – a labourer.'

'Where does he live?'

'Three Sneinton Terrace.'

'What did the two of you do?'

'Discussed bikes and things.'

'And when did you leave him?'

'Maybe half-past four. I'd got back to the house and left again by five.'

'Did you actually see your uncle dead?'

'No. I was going to try something else if Henry didn't come up with the goods.' He faced Montgomery with an air of bravado, but his fingers gripped each other tightly. 'You see, it's all straightforward,' he said. 'I'm ready to make a statement now.'

'Are you? What makes you think we want one?'

Martin's jaw dropped. 'You *must* want one! I've told you everything! I'm guilty!'

'So you say.'

Martin drew himself up in the chair. 'I have a *criminal record*,' he announced.

'We know.'

'You *must* charge me,' he said earnestly.

'Oh – we might. You can sample our Hospitality Suite while

91

we check out your story, and then perhaps you will be charged. Wasting police time is a criminal offence.'

Martin flushed. 'There's no need to check anything out. I'll sign now.'

'There's every need. Sergeant Bird – please will you take another officer and accompany Mr Witherspoon downstairs? Thank you.' He left the room.

Ten minutes later, Montgomery and Sergeant Bird met up again.

'Pack of lies,' said Sergeant Bird.

'Yes. A few hours in a cell should cool him off nicely – but *why* has he done this?'

'Seeking attention.'

'Possibly – but I didn't get that feel.'

'Maybe he's angling for approval from his parents, by martyring himself.'

'But why should they approve of a confession of murder? No – he's shielding someone, and I think I know who.'

'The mother.'

'You noticed it, too? She's an odd one, that woman. Stood almost catatonic while we took him away. Perhaps she was in shock, but I would have expected *some* protest . . .'

'Supposing he only *thinks* she did it: he gave the motive hesitantly, and it would fit her rather than him . . . if he was wrong, she probably believes it was him, hence her lack of reaction.'

Montgomery grimaced. 'We're hovering on the threshold of total confusion,' he said. 'Only facts will sort the wheat from the chaff, so I propose we find Ray Cooper while Martin has no opportunity to prime him.'

11

Ray Cooper took some tracking down. Eventually they located him in the deafening moonscape of a building site, swathed in floury dust and instinctive hostility.

'An incident occurred last Saturday,' explained Montgomery. 'We don't think Martin was involved, but we need to pinpoint his movements in order to establish that beyond doubt. Did you see him at all?'

Ray screwed up his eyes, considering what response would serve Martin best. He was lean and tanned, with a snake tattooed across his right shoulder.

'Yeah,' he said at last. 'He came round to our place about two o'clock.'

'Sneinton Terrace?'

'Yeah.'

'How long did he stay?'

'Not long; maybe twenty minutes. I was going to buy some gear in town, and he was going to see some old man. We set off together on our bikes.'

'Where did you part company?'

'The old man's place.'

'Where is that?'

'I dunno the address, but I could show you. It's near the railway line.'

They returned to the car and drove to his direction. As flat grey factories and tired terraces gave way to rows of modest but generally well-kept bungalows, Ray Cooper leaned forward from the back seat.

'That one – no, that one. Yeah!' He pointed forcefully

through the windscreen, and a rank armpit passed inches from Montgomery's face.

'Thank you,' said Montgomery, opening the electric window with an air of nonchalance. 'Did you actually see the old man yourself?'

'Yeah. He came out as Martin turned into his drive.'

They chauffeured Ray back to his building site, parked near the bungalow and approached it on foot. The paintwork was weathered and flaking, but the small square front garden was vivid with dahlias and neatly pruned rose bushes including a favourite of Sergeant Bird's, the orange-yellow 'Glenfiddich'. A background drone of bees accompanied their brief progress up the drive.

The main entrance was at the side. Montgomery rang the bell and waited, aware that an elderly lady was peering at him from the house next door.

'Do you think Mr Cooper is having us on?' murmured Sergeant Bird.

'He'd better not be – ah!'

There was a shuffling sound, and the door opened to reveal a sinewy man of advanced years and few teeth.

'Hello?' he said.

'Police,' said Montgomery, showing his warrant card with discretion. 'May we come in for a moment?'

'Yes. Let me just tell my wife. Hilda! There are two police-men here!'

He led the way into a cramped but cosily furnished sitting-room, and introduced himself as Walter Lampkin. His wife, an overweight woman who sat knitting babies' bootees – yellow to cover all options – smiled at them affably. She wore thick stockings despite the summer heat.

'How can we help you?'

'Do you know a Martin Witherspoon?'

'Yes! He comes here on Saturdays. A good lad is Martin.'

'Was he here last Saturday?'

'He was.'

'What time did he arrive and when did he leave?'

'He came at a quarter past two, as usual, and left – oh, I suppose it was five o'clock. Is that right, dear?'

'Yes.' The plump lady had put down her knitting and was gazing at Montgomery in surprise. 'Why are you asking questions about Martin?' she asked. 'Is he in some sort of trouble?'

'No. We're just trying to eliminate him from our enquiries.'

'Oh, that's all right then. Whoever you're after can't be him anyway – he's such a helpful boy.'

'What exactly does he do here?'

The old man took up the tale. 'He digs for us on the allotment. I can't do much these days, even though I'd like to, because of angina – the old ticker, you know. I had a bit of a heart attack once; a warning, the doctor said. And Hilda can't help because of her thrombosis.'

'I potter with the secateurs,' she said.

'Are the Witherspoons friends of the family?' asked Sergeant Bird.

'No – though we regard Martin as a friend now. We put an advert in the *Recorder*, asking if someone could give us an hour or two of gardening for a small sum, and Martin saw it. He won't let us pay him, though; he says Hilda's chicken sandwiches are worth their weight in gold!'

They both chuckled, and Montgomery struggled with a feeling of unreality. This was not what he had expected. 'Was he definitely here all afternoon?' he asked. 'Did he leave at all, even for a few minutes?'

'No – he was here. I was in the allotment with him, and Stan next door was doing his patch, so he can tell you. The sun was burning down; Stan's wife brought us all a glass of homemade lemonade.'

'I see; well – '

'Do come and look. I've got some grand runner beans. It's only at the bottom of the garden.'

Without waiting for their answer, he walked into the kitchen, obliging them to follow. Outside was a tiny lawn with flower borders, and below this the ground fell away towards the railway cutting in a patchwork of allotments. In the distance they could see the black maw of a tunnel. 'I'm lucky,' said Mr Lampkin. 'Mine's right next to the bungalow. Now look at these . . . I've got onions and carrots, potatoes, leeks, peas – and here are the beans. Yes, they're white-flowered ones; they don't go stringy so quickly as the scarlet. You eat them young and tender. The secret's in the mulching, you know. Stan gives me his grass cuttings, 'cause I haven't enough of my own. In return he has all the beans he needs. We help each other in this neighbourhood.'

A man emerged from a shed in the adjoining allotment.

'Is this Stan?' asked Montgomery.

'It is indeed. Stan, these gentlemen are policemen. They want to know where Martin was on Saturday afternoon. You tell them.'

'Why, here!' said Stan. His look of surprise changed into a knowing grin. 'You're after a bikey-boy, is that it? They all look the same with those crash helmets on. Well, it won't be Martin you want; he's a real credit to British youth.'

Hilda Lampkin was still knitting when they returned to the bungalow.

'Nice of you to have called,' she said.

'You must have these,' insisted her husband, thrusting an enormous brown paper bag full of runner beans towards Montgomery.

'I – aren't they for someone else?'

'I picked them for the lady over the road, but we've plenty more for her. You have them – and give some to Mr Bird. You're welcome to come again, any time.'

The parcel lay on the back seat as they drove back to the station. For some reason he couldn't identify, it made Montgomery feel uncomfortable.

'Are you off home, Will?' asked Montgomery at the end of the afternoon.

'Yes, if there's nothing else you want me for.'

'See you tomorrow.'

Montgomery serenely updated his report, rang Carole, then gathered up his belongings. He was going to pay a call on Katherine Adams at the Venning Road surgery. It would be a low-key, semi-official visit, best handled alone; Sergeant Bird, for all his virtues, looked every inch the policeman.

He told himself that his choice had fallen on Dr Adams because the others were too intimately involved with the Witherspoons – and this was true. Nevertheless, he knew that an additional element had influenced his decision: her appearance attracted him, and he wanted to meet her. His colleagues would have found this most surprising; indeed, he surprised himself. In the course of his work his manner was habitually punctilious, sexless as a eunuch. He loved Carole and was totally faithful to her. Yet one glimpse of Katherine Adams's dark beauty had stirred in him a deep and subtle hunger for more . . .

Evening surgery had almost ended when Montgomery was instructed to take a seat near the pile of magazines and box of toys. Instead, he wandered up the corridor and loitered near the door of Dr Adams's room. Voices murmured both inside and opposite, where a door-plate read 'Sister Tarrant'.

The nurse practitioner's door opened first, and a young man came out clutching his upper arm. The uniformed woman just behind him called: 'Enjoy your holiday!' then turned as if to go back into the room.

'Excuse me,' Montgomery said rapidly.

'Yes?'

'My name's Montgomery . . . CID. I'm hoping to see Dr Adams shortly, but I wonder if I could have a word with you first?'

'Of course. Is it about Neville's mother?'

'Yes.'

'It's *so* upsetting for him. That, and then his daughter . . . Come this way. We've got a little tea-room and there's no one in it at present. If we keep the door ajar, you won't miss Dr Adams. Will you have a cup?'

As she busied herself with the kettle, he asked careful questions about the practice. 'Have you worked here long, Sister?'

'Fifteen years. My children are quite grown up now.'

'Is it congenial?'

'Oh yes. I love meeting people, and this is a well-run practice. I hope it'll be as nice when Dr Quested retires.'

'Is that definite?'

'Well, he'll have to when he's seventy. They used to be able to go on and on, but now there's a limit. It's only right, really. Doctors start losing their faculties like everyone else. But we'll all miss Dr Quested. He's such a gentleman. Never rude or impatient. Neither is Dr Adams. But the other two have their off-days.'

'What are they like as colleagues?'

'I can't complain. They're very competent, keep decent records and usually communicate well. But I wish Dr Witherspoon had just a glimmer of a sense of humour; he takes everything *so* seriously. And sometimes his anger can be so cold it makes you shudder.'

'Is the work of the practice shared equally?'

Sister Tarrant took a deep breath. 'No,' she said. 'In my view, Dr Adams has to do far too much. A lot of the patients like a lady doctor, and of course she willingly sees them, but they remain registered with one of the men. Her clinics are often twice as long as theirs. And the medical student we've got – that was Dr Forester's idea. He thought it would bring prestige to the practice. But he goes off freely on his jaunts, and others have to do the actual teaching. Dr Quested likes cosy chats with Jonathan in the tea-room, then it's Dr Adams he spends the rest of the day with.'

'Does this cause bad blood?'

'Not on the surface. Underneath, I can't say. Dr Adams shares the odd grumble with me in the Ladies Room – we act as safety-valves for one another – but that's more for the trivial annoyances. I don't know what she thinks about long-term situations. She's very self-contained.'

'Is there a Mr Adams?'

'Not now. She's divorced.'

'Ah. Children?'

'No.'

Montgomery took another sip of tea. 'Regarding children,' he said, 'do Neville's children ever call in here – to look round, or meet their father?'

'Yes,' said Sister Tarrant. 'Deborah came a few weeks ago. We showed her all the clinical rooms, and our little dispensary, but I think she liked the toys in the waiting-room best!'

98

'What about Martin?'

'No. I've never seen him here. I only met him once, in fact, at a cocktail party Neville gave. The party wasn't a success, unfortunately; it never warmed up, if you know what I mean. Lynn was obviously struggling with the role of hostess, and Katherine, who perhaps could have helped, had another engagement.'

'What was your impression of Martin?'

'Oh – I didn't see enough of him to say. He sneaked out after half an hour, and roared away on his bike.'

At that moment, Katherine Adams's door opened across the corridor, and two figures emerged.

'Thanks for all your help,' said Montgomery quickly, and hastened to catch the GP before she reached the reception area.

'Dr Adams?'

She turned round with an interrogative look, and he saw that her skin was a smooth magnolia and her brown hair was glossy as mink.

'Yes?' she asked.

'My name's Richard Montgomery,' he said. 'Detective Inspector. Could you spare me a few minutes?'

She looked at her watch. 'Yes – perhaps fifteen. I'm due at the Theatre Royal at half past seven.'

'Thank you. I won't keep you. I'm checking a few points about the recent deaths in Doctor Witherspoon's family, and the disappearance of his daughter Deborah.'

'Poor little girl; she must be very confused.'

Montgomery nodded. 'Have you met both the children?'

'Yes. Neville introduced me to Martin once in town, and Deborah sometime﹄ visits the practice.'

'Not Martin?'

'No. I gather Martin has never shown an interest in medicine, which has been a disappointment to Neville.'

'I suppose it's a pleasant tradition to have another doctor in the family.'

Katherine Adams gave a cool smile. 'Neville would certainly wish to comply with tradition.'

'Is the drug warfarin freely available from chemists' shops?'

'Not without prescription.'

'Do you have it in your dispensary?'

'Yes, we do.'

'Would it be easy to find?'

She raised her well-marked eyebrows. 'It's under "W" on the shelf.'

'What about those free samples that the drug reps bring you? Might there be warfarin among those?'

'Oh, no. That would be quite inappropriate. Warfarin is a valuable but potentially dangerous drug, which is prescribed for a patient in conjunction with regular hospital blood tests. Pharmaceutical representatives leave us medicines such as painkillers, antihistamines or antacids, which we can invite patients to try if they aren't getting adequate relief with established medicines. These can be entirely new drugs, or different formulations of existing ones, such as a gel for rubbing into painful muscles.'

'I see. But you said your dispensary stocks warfarin?'

'Yes.'

'Why do you have a dispensary here?'

'A lot of our catchment area is rural, and the people have no access to a pharmacy.'

'Ah – so if a patient is actually bedridden, you as a doctor could bring the appropriate tablets with you when you visit.'

'Yes.'

'May I see the dispensary?'

'Certainly.'

It was a neat, white-painted little anteroom set back from the main corridor next to Reception. A counter blocked access from the corridor itself, but the dispensary had two doors, one leading into an adjoining clinical room, the other connecting directly with Reception. There were shelves of drugs, a fridge and a computer for labelling and stock control.

'What happens to the completed prescriptions?' asked Montgomery.

'The filled ones are handed straight to the patient, or kept on this shelf near the counter.'

'Mm. Is there always someone in here?'

'Not always.'

'Is that safe?'

'Well, the dispensary is very public, and of course it's locked after hours.'

Montgomery glanced at his watch. Three more minutes. 'Do you like your colleagues, Dr Adams? Would you outline them for me?'

She smiled. 'Dr Quested is a charming man, Dr Forester has many enthusiasms, and Dr Witherspoon is – diligent in his way.'

'What about Lynn Witherspoon?'

'I hardly know her.'

'Has she visited the surgery recently?'

'Socially, you mean? No; we see much more of Trudi Forester – but then, she has a car and Lynn hasn't.'

'I see. Well, thank you for your time, Dr Adams. I hope you enjoy the play.'

She held out her hand, and the clasp they shared was firm and friendly. 'Thank *you*, Inspector Montgomery. I wish you well with your investigations.'

They walked out of the surgery together, and Katherine Adams paused by her blue Renault 25 to address him once more. For the first time, shades of urgency coloured her tone.

'You'll keep looking for Deborah, won't you?' she said. 'I don't know why she ran away, but it must have been a mistake. Neville is heartbroken. Tell me if there's anything I can do . . .'

Montgomery assured her he would, and watched as she drove away with crisp, decisive movements.

Deborah . . . He had started off that afternoon with his mind full of Martin, yet now it was his sister who haunted him from her place of hiding: Deborah, fifteen, that transitional age between child and woman; Deborah from an unhappy home where two people had died mysteriously; Deborah, fleeing because of a threat to the life of her cat, possibly the only creature she loved without reservation in that repressive household . . .

Was that truly the reason she had left? Or was she running away from something more terrible?

12

The evening was well advanced as Montgomery rang the bell at the Witherspoons' house. His thin mouth curved into a shadowy smile; let Martin wonder if he was about to spend the night in a police cell!

Neville himself opened the door and eagerly ushered his visitor into the lounge, where Lynn eyed them gravely. Once seated, Montgomery began to reiterate the main points of Martin's story; at the mention of crushed warfarin tablets in tea, Neville could contain himself no longer.

'It's quite fantastic!' he exploded. 'Unbelievable. I don't know why he's saying this; I can't understand it.'

'What are your reservations?' asked Montgomery. He had carefully avoided revealing the time Martin claimed to have administered the poison; the acquisition of unbiased information about the household's culinary habits was of paramount necessity.

Neville bridled. 'Where does one start? I know nothing of the solubility of warfarin, but I do know that Martin hardly ever took tea in to Mother. And where does he claim to have got hold of the drug? You can't buy it over the counter like sweets!'

'He said it came from your surgery.'

'Not there.' There was pain in the doctor's face. 'No, not there – wait!' He seemed to recollect something. 'That isn't possible. Martin has never been in the surgery. I'm afraid he's never shown any leanings towards medicine.'

'What about as a patient?'

'Lynn and the children are registered with Dr Bell in town.

102

He's always been Lynn's GP, so it seemed proper for the children to consult him too.'

'But Deborah has visited your practice?'

'Yes. The last time was two or three months ago. I was gratified by her interest.'

'Can you remember if she saw any of the drug samples brought to you by the representatives?'

'It's possible – yes, I believe she did. That's right, I showed her the cupboard where I keep them. But Inspector, you wouldn't find warfarin in such a place.'

'I know. Returning for a moment to the tea, are you both positive that Martin didn't attend his grandmother in the mornings, for instance?'

'Yes,' said Neville. 'We had enough trouble trying to make him eat a proper breakfast himself. Tea for Mother was always Deborah's job.'

'Did he administer anything at all to Maud that week?'

Neville turned to Lynn, and her forehead creased. 'It's difficult to remember now,' she murmured. 'Just her lunch on the Wednesday, I think – fruit crumble and custard; he came home that day to catch a programme on television.'

'Nothing on Thursday?'

'No.'

'Please can you tell me exactly who visited Maud that week?'

'Well, I'll try. There was Dr Quested, of course ... Mrs Weddell Grant – '

'When?' demanded Montgomery.

'Wednesday afternoon. She stayed about two hours. Then there were three ladies from the LFG on Thursday afternoon; we told you about them before.'

'Anybody else?'

'No.'

'Did anyone from the practice come on Dr Quested's behalf – to bring medicines, perhaps?'

'No.'

Five people, then, apart from the family – and in cases of poisoning, family always had optimal opportunity. Montgomery looked at Lynn Witherspoon's face and tried to unlock the cipher of those opaque features, but it was no good; all he could detect was stubbornness, and glimpses of a hostility which may or may not have been directed towards him.

What had Deborah done? Or what did she know? Did she suspect her mother, and find the whole situation impossible to cope with? What did the parents themselves think?

'Moving on to George's death,' he said, 'Martin says he returned to the house at half past four, picked up Henry and put him in the dining-room. We know from the forensic examination that George was dead before three, so Martin's story has to be false. We also have witnesses who were in Martin's company for the whole afternoon.'

Neville sighed, and shook his head wearily. 'It's nonsense anyway,' he said. 'Henry would never let Martin near him. They didn't get on.'

'Martin said nothing about catmint, either,' added Montgomery, and saw Lynn's lips compress. He decided to drive home the circumstances of George's death and extract their own theories on the matter.

'Just remind me about the cat,' he said. 'He was definitely in the conservatory when you all left the house? Yes. And there are three doors between the conservatory and the dining-room? Right . . . Could he possibly have passed through those three doorways under his own steam?'

'No,' said Neville. 'The doors were firmly shut; we checked.'

'What about the window, then? Might your brother have needed air and opened it, only for Henry to jump in at him?'

'No. There were a lot of pollens about – I could feel them myself. George wouldn't go into the garden at all, and he kept his bedroom window tightly closed. He'd never have opened the dining-room one.'

'I see. Yet Henry *did* get inside the room. How do you think that happened?'

Neville and Lynn exchanged unhappy glances.

'We don't know,' he said. 'We've really no idea.'

'Deborah ran away that very evening,' went on Montgomery, aware that he was about to tread delicate ground. 'Do you think *she* might have seen something – or know something?'

Lynn's blank face bunched into ridges of anger. 'I resent that suggestion!' she said loudly. 'Deborah was out. What can she know? It might just as well have been the person George spoke to on the phone, or one of our neighbours, as Deborah!'

Montgomery was instantly alert. 'What's this?' he asked. 'I thought the telephone was kept in the hall, which was why George couldn't summon help when he was taken ill.'

'It is, normally, but the phone is portable; we simply keep the base plate in the hall. George must have asked one of the children to bring him the receiver.'

'And that was replaced when he finished?'

'Yes. I took it to make a call myself.'

'Who did he ring, Mrs Witherspoon?'

'I don't know. He didn't seem to have many friends; that was the only call I heard him make from the house.'

'Can you remember what he said?'

'It was only the tail end of the conversation. He spoke of a letter he had sent, and invited the person to visit. He also asked them to think about something; I assumed he meant the visit.'

'Were any names at all mentioned?'

'No; I'm sorry.'

'Perhaps he had an address book. Would you allow me to see his room?'

'Yes, if it helps.'

'And maybe I could look upstairs as well, if you don't mind?'

She hesitated.

'Of course, Inspector,' said Neville heartily.

'Thank you.'

George's room was tidily arranged, no doubt by Lynn. Two suitcases stood in the corner, flanked by small boxes of oddments.

'I put his books and stationery in that one,' said Lynn, pointing.

Montgomery lifted out the contents in a stack, and replaced them one by one. When he came to a dog-eared yellowing notepad, he examined it closely. Sheets had been torn off, probably over the years; he held the pad obliquely in the light, and saw indentations.

'I'll take this, with your permission,' he said, sliding it into a plastic bag. 'It might tell us to whom George last wrote.' An idea occurred to him: 'If he wasn't very mobile, he must have given his letters to one of the family to post. Can either of you remember any details of recipients?'

'I've posted nothing,' said Lynn. Her manner was quite animated now that the focus of attention had moved away from her immediate family nucleus. 'Perhaps Deborah took it for him.'

Deborah's own correspondence was a source of some contention, remembered Montgomery. It seemed to be out of character for the girl to run off without leaving even a hastily scrawled note, and he disliked facts that didn't fit. When he moved upstairs to examine her room, he spent some time on hands and knees in case a paper had fluttered out of sight.

'We've already looked,' said Lynn. 'She must have been in a terrible hurry. But why hasn't she *telephoned*?'

Montgomery was working his way through Deborah's desk. 'Where does she keep her personal stationery?' he asked.

'She usually borrows mine,' said Lynn, 'but we gave her a box for her last birthday. It's here, still in its cellophane.'

'Mmm ... ' He rummaged further, then began to flick through the school exercise books he had removed from the desk. In one, which contained neat lists of physics formulae, he saw fragments of paper trapped by the staples at the spine, indicating that at least one double page had been torn out. Casually, he added this book to his haul before they crossed the corridor to Martin's room.

It was inhibiting to be overlooked so closely as he searched, especially when he didn't really know what he was looking for, but suddenly Montgomery had a piece of luck. The telephone rang: both Witherspoons descended to the hall and he was given almost ten minutes of freedom while voices murmured below.

He wanted to form a mental picture of Martin, as indeed of every member of this household. What were his hobbies, his interests? He suspected that Neville would be unable to describe them.

Martin's clothes ranged from worn leathers to a smart beige suit in thin material; his books were Westerns and thrillers, plus a few copies of a popular biking magazine. The inevitable soft pornography was well hidden under the bed, but Lynn surely knew about it.

Montgomery was on the point of straightening up when he saw a rim of newsprint below the highly coloured magazines. He reached out and extricated three copies of the Nottingham *Recorder*, the most recent dated a month before. Idly he turned the pages, wondering why Martin had kept these; in a column headed 'Helpline', where individuals wrote of items lost and found, or solicited contributions for their jumble sales, a blue asterisk identified the answer: a Mr Lampkin required assistance with his garden.

Quickly Montgomery searched out the 'Helpline' in the older papers; two similar appeals were marked, and he jotted down the details in his notebook. Just in time – the Witherspoons were ascending the stairs again.

They spoke of Deborah before he left to authorize Martin's release, and it occurred to Montgomery that 'Helpline' would be a good place to advertise for the missing cat.

'Dr Witherspoon,' he said in a low voice as Lynn retreated to the kitchen, 'may I ask you about the scar above Martin's eye? I believe Deborah caused the injury.'

The doctor's reluctant nod confirmed Montgomery's suspicion, so he continued: 'How did she do it?'

'Is this relevant? The incident was years ago.'

'It could be.'

'Very well . . . she flew at him with the hedge clippers.'

At ten o'clock Lynn heard the kitchen door bang, and watched Neville rise to his feet as if someone had just activated his clockwork. He disappeared into the hall; she heard his voice, and then Martin's.

Slowly she put down the magazine she had been attempting to read. She began to walk to the door, but somehow it was

too difficult and she stopped in the middle of the room. Martin
... What was there to say? Why had he done what he did,
unless ... ? At least the police had let him go.

She caught sight of her face in a mirror; it was strange and
blank. Now the voices were louder, and she couldn't shut out
the words:

'You can't stop me! I'm nearly nineteen now, and I can go
where I like! Don't pretend you aren't glad!'

'But this is your home. Where will you go?'

'I'll doss down with Ray; you can contact me there. Give me
five minutes to get my things, then you'll have no more
problems.'

'But Martin ... son ...'

The thump of feet on the stair treads was the only answer to
that, and Lynn's gaze swivelled to the ceiling as creaks and
scrapes from the floor above signalled Martin's contemptuous
preparations to leave. Her brain was set in ice; the image in the
mirror gripped its own arms as if in a fierce hug, yet she felt
nothing.

More voices, more feet, more doors; the shocking din of a
motor-cycle engine ...

Neville came into the room. His shoulders slumped deject-
edly and his mouth was white and pinched, yet his eyes
assessed her with their old cold fire.

'I hope you're satisfied,' he said. 'I hope you're happy now.
You've finally got what you wanted.'

13

The most immediate side-effect of the warfarin discovery was the doubling of Montgomery's small task force, expediting the collation of useful information.

'Smythe and I have interviewed those three biddies who witnessed the alteration to the will,' said Brian Jackson as detectives crowded into the inspector's office. 'They're all old, and we reckon that even in their heyday their local Mensa branch was never in danger of oversubscription. Only one of them "thought it was a bit odd" to change the thrust of a will so radically on the same paper, rather than making an entirely new one. Mrs Witherspoon told her that it was to save re-writing all the other provisions – the small bequests, etc., which were to stay the same. She called it a kind of codicil, and the three witnesses were satisfied.'

Montgomery nodded, feeling a grim admiration for Maud Witherspoon. He was as near certain as he could be that the old woman had wilfully manipulated her three guests that Thursday and, through them, Gertrude Weddell Grant.

'We brought samples of their handwriting, as you suggested,' added Smythe, holding out a slender sheaf of papers. Montgomery took them, and briefly assessed them by eye. One hand was a careful copperplate, the others were childishly rounded; none resembled the characteristic penmanship of the anonymous letter-writer, but only an expert could tell him for certain.

'Thanks,' he said. 'Anyone got anything else?'

William Bird, the last to enter, had been longing to speak. 'I have,' he said. 'I've just been in contact with Forensic, and their Document Examiner has processed the notepad you took from George's room. You'll be pleased to hear that those indentations represent a one-page letter which was almost entirely legible. An official report's on its way, but I've made a copy of what they told me.' He opened his notebook. 'The date was July the second – that's the Sunday before he died – and the address was Oaklands. George wrote: *Dear Evie, you've probably heard that I've got a billet with Neville now. I wish you'd come and see me, give me another chance. I know my flat wasn't fit for a lady. Don't worry about Lynn. If you come next Saturday afternoon, she'll be out. They're all going out. Send me a letter, Evie, or just turn up. Make a poor old sailor happy. Ever yours, George. P.S. There's a spare back door key hanging behind the hose-pipe to the right of the garage.*'

'Well!' said Montgomery. 'What more could we ask for! He actually invited her to the house *on that Saturday afternoon!*'

'And rang to check up on her, presumably because he'd heard nothing all week,' finished William Bird.

'That would explain his choice of seat, too. The lounge was undoubtedly the most comfortable room in the house, yet George chose the Parker Knoll near the dining-room window because it gave such an excellent view of the driveway. For those of you who don't know the geography, the main door is in the south side wall.'

'So he was watching out for Evie,' said Jackson. 'Who is she?'

'That's the question, isn't it? And what does that reference to Lynn mean?' Montgomery felt instinctively that he must speak with Neville alone.

'Is the drive the only access to the house?' asked Smythe, eyes animated in his oddly poetic face.

'A narrow path leads into the woodlands behind,' said Montgomery. 'It links up with a track the locals call the "back lane", which skirts the hill and eventually comes out on the fringes of the Clarkwood Estate. An intruder could have reached the house that way, and gone right round past the conservatory and morning-room to reach the kitchen door unobserved. We think Deborah may have taken that route in reverse when she left: the other end of the lane comes out by a farmyard only fifty yards from Thorbeck's telephone box.' He turned to William Bird. 'Forensic have done well with that letter. Did they have any joy with Deborah's physics notebook?'

'Sorry, sir. There was nothing useful on the remaining pages. If she *did* write a note, the middle pages weren't *in situ* at the time. The lab checked the front and back covers as well, in case she'd torn out the double sheet, then rested it on the notebook itself, but there was no result.'

'I suppose we can't win them all. Right, then . . .'

The informal briefing broke up, and the officers wandered off to continue their lines of investigation.

William Bird lingered. 'Where do you think she is, sir?' he asked. Despite his status as a longstanding family friend, he always called Montgomery 'sir'.

'I wish I knew.' Montgomery walked to the window; outside, the sun was attempting to break through an overcast sky. 'If she was any other teenage girl, we'd be liaising with the Met by now. But I don't feel she's gone as far as London. There'd be no place for Henry there, and she wouldn't abandon him.'

'Her resources must be expended.'

'Yes. I'll be honest, Will – I'm worried. By all accounts, Deborah isn't streetwise. Unless some friend or mentor is looking out for her, unpleasant things may happen.' He stared at his sergeant's rosy face, and saw that he understood not only the fears expressed but that which had remained unsaid . . . If Deborah was desperate enough for reasons unconnected with Henry, then the harm might not only come from others.

The telephone on Montgomery's desk shrilled; he answered it, detaining William Bird with a gesture.

A warm, faintly brassy voice came down the line: 'Inspector Montgomery, it's Mrs Blanchard here – Aileen's mother. I rang your switchboard and they said I could talk to you directly. Is it all right?'

'Perfectly.'

'I remembered something that might help in your search for Deborah. It's just an outside chance, but there's a place where she may have taken Henry . . . Last year one of our neighbours showed Aileen her new kitten, and said she'd got it from a Cat Rescue Centre run by an eccentric lady out near Papplewick. It's not a registered charity, and it isn't in the Yellow Pages either, but it's run from a smallholding with a funny name – something like Smiling Don.'

'That's very helpful. Did Aileen remind you of this, Mrs Blanchard?'

'No, I thought of it myself. But she told me about it last year, and I'm fairly sure Deborah knew as well. I've asked Aileen today, but she says she's forgotten the details.'

'I see. Can you tell me the name or address of the neighbour with the kitten?'

'I'm sorry; they moved.'

'Never mind. I think that's enough for us to go on. Thank you for taking the trouble to ring. If anything else comes to mind, even if you're not sure of its value, do contact us. We'd be very pleased to hear from you.'

He put down the telephone after the final courtesies and conveyed the gist of the call to Sergeant Bird.

'So we want a farmhouse or smallholding with a name like "Smiling Don", in the general area of Papplewick,' he finished up. He reached for the Yellow Pages, checked through the list of farmers without much hope, and gave a small shake of the head. The ordinary telephone directory was similarly uninformative.

'Don't worry.' said Sergeant Bird. 'The local postman will know.'

Smilodon proved to be a collection of ramshackle buildings nestling between brilliant yellow fields of oilseed rape on the outskirts of Papplewick. A narrow track, pitted with craters and hostile with stones, wound its way uphill to end in a junction with a fissured concrete courtyard.

'One has to be motivated to come up here,' muttered Montgomery, hanging on to his seat-belt as Sergeant Bird manoeuvred their police Metro between the worst of the craters.

He recalled the bicycle belonging to the postman who had just directed them, and winced. 'There's no need to grin. What does "Smilodon" mean anyway?'

'It's the proper name for the sabre-toothed tiger.'

'You would know that.'

They parked on the soundest-looking portion of concrete, and alighted from the car. The nearest building, a small barn, was empty, so they walked up to the house itself and knocked on the door.

'Round the side,' called an imperious voice.

Montgomery and his sergeant exchanged glances and set off towards the source of the sound. As they turned the corner of the house, they saw row upon row of wire enclosures, each with a feline resident. The compounds stretched round to the back of the house and were sheltered by its bulk on one side and a stone wall on the other. Behind the wall leaned an uneven row of poplars.

'I hope you've come for a kitten,' said the voice. 'There are seventeen here looking for homes.'

A stout woman of about sixty emerged from a nearby door, carrying an empty bucket which she deposited beneath an outside tap. She wore a green wool cardigan over a grey blouse, trousers of suspiciously masculine design, and wellington boots. Her iron-grey hair was short and straight, a geometric frame for her weather-beaten face, yet the blue eyes held a kindly sparkle.

Montgomery introduced himself and his sergeant.

'Pity,' was her reaction. 'I don't suppose you want a cat, then. I'm Felicity Goodridge. What can I do for you?'

'We're looking for a young girl who's been missing from her home since last Saturday evening. She left with a nine-year-old ginger tom who had been the cause of some trouble because she believed her parents were going to get rid of him. We wondered if anyone had brought such a cat to you within the last week – asking for temporary boarding, perhaps?'

'A young girl, you said. About twenty?'

'Deborah is fifteen.'

'What is the name of the cat?'

'Henry.'

Miss Goodridge gave a small nod, as if of comprehension. 'I believe I can help you,' she said. 'Come this way.'

She led them past the compounds and as she did, the occupants seemed to come alive: they ran to the front, gazing at her adoringly, some mewing for attention. Montgomery noticed that each had a good-sized run, a high platform to sit on, a sheltered area of bedding and toys to play with. For all the general disrepair of the premises, no effort had been spared to make the cats comfortable.

Only the animals in the two end compounds isolated themselves from the euphoria; one, a short-haired black and white cat, gave no response at all while the other, a hulking ginger tom, peered at them suspiciously over the edge of his platform.

'A girl appeared here on Sunday morning,' said their guide. 'She told me she had come to the area because her grandmother was ill, and the old lady had just gone into hospital for a fortnight. She said she couldn't stay to look after the cat, and asked if I would take him. Apparently the local catteries were full. I requested a contact address, and she gave me one – it's in Worcestershire. This is the cat she brought.' She indicated the huge ginger tom.

'He was well cared for, with a flea collar but no name tag. I asked his name. She hesitated, said "George" and then went very white. I thought she was going to faint. She apologized, and told me she had been too busy to eat; I insisted she had some toast before she left.'

'Was this your visitor?' asked Montgomery, handing over a photograph of Deborah.

Felicity Goodridge gave the picture a thorough scrutiny. 'I can't be positive,' she said. 'This is a schoolgirl; the young woman I saw wore immaculate make-up and a hat. Her hair was in a neat bun. I had assessed her as a shy twenty-year-old. Yet the jawline is similar – the nose too . . . yes; it could be.'

Again she turned towards the compound. 'I knew this cat wasn't called George. He has never shown the slightest response to the name. Over the week I've tried him with several: only "Benny" met with a flicker of interest. Now I can understand why.'

114

Montgomery stared at the cat inside. 'May I?' he asked quietly.

'Of course.'

He slid aside the metal strip which barred the door and stepped warily into the enclosure. The occupant sitting high at the back watched him with equal circumspection. Montgomery had been shown photographs of Henry at the Witherspoons' house; certainly this cat bore a strong resemblance, but Montgomery was not a great cat lover, and to him most ginger toms looked the same. He halted three feet away from the animal.

'George,' he whispered. Not a whisker moved.

'Henry.' The ears sprang up alertly and recognition gleamed from the amber eyes.

'Henry,' he repeated. 'You know your name, don't you, lad?' He held up his hand, but changed his mind as the large cat stirred and looked about him eagerly, as if seeking a person he knew. His tense attitude, high on the platform, gave strong reminder of his feral ancestry, making Montgomery feel nervous; never mind Smiling Don – to him all cats were potentially snarling Dons with those claws and long sharp teeth. He slowly retreated to the front of the pen.

'Henry,' he called, crouching down. 'Ch-ch-ch-ch.'

Henry rose to his feet with a grace which belied his bulk, padded down the ramp and approached Montgomery. After carefully sniffing his hand and the lower edges of his trousers, he grudgingly allowed himself to be stroked. Montgomery, for his part, much preferred this situation where he could look down on the cat. Henry was plump and sleek, with rich ginger fur and a brindled tail. Only a tiny white 'bib' interrupted the overall colouring. His face was benignly leonine, and under Montgomery's tentative ministrations he had actually begun to purr.

It was bizarre to think that this animal had been used as a murder weapon. Montgomery had known of babies accidentally smothered by household pets, but never an adult killed deliberately. Yet George's anguished face was seldom far from recall, neither was the image conjured up by Neville's story –

that of a ginger cat called Henry lying on the body, purring. Just as he was doing now.

'It's him all right, sir.' Sergeant Bird's voice, so normal, came as a slight shock.

'I agree,' said Montgomery, swiftly controlling his imagination. 'Now, how do I get out of here without Henry following?'

'Roll that pink ball to the back of his quarters,' suggested Miss Goodridge. 'It has catmint inside; he'll chase it.'

Montgomery took the advice, first allowing Henry a preliminary sniff at the ball. Seconds later he stood outside in the yard.

'Why is the black and white cat so listless?' asked Sergeant Bird as they began to walk back towards the house.

'Oh, that's Sam,' said their hostess. 'He's been here for four months. His owner was an old gentleman who died, and Sam's fairly long in the tooth himself – I'd say ten at least. People want kittens, naturally, just as they prefer to adopt babies. The older members of the species come low on the list. I try to give all my cats attention, Sam included, but what he really needs is a quiet home, perhaps with another old person or couple.'

She led the way through the doorway from which she had first emerged, and the detectives found themselves in a utility room. Faint scuffling sounds emanated from a cardboard box standing in the corner alongside a pair of ancient brogues.

'Have a look,' invited Miss Goodridge.

They leaned over; inside, a tabby queen lay with six squirming kittens.

'Delightful, aren't they?' she said. 'That's our latest litter. You wonder how anyone could maltreat such creatures. But too many people want novelty, not responsibility. I do my best to check the credentials of any prospective owners.' She opened the kitchen door. 'In here are eleven more. If any of your colleagues – *responsible persons* – should be seeking a pet, please ask them to contact me.'

'Do you run this centre single-handedly?' asked Montgomery.

'Not quite. A friend of mine who is a vet gives his services

116

free of charge, and supplies me with medicines to treat the more straightforward ailments myself. He places advertisements in his waiting-room, and word of mouth brings other interested parties. Perhaps that's how you found Smilodon?'

'Yes . . . ' Montgomery mentioned the kitten on the Clarkwood Estate, and the conversation reverted to Deborah. Unfortunately she had given no hint of her local lodgings; the Worcestershire address, which Miss Goodridge briskly copied down for them, was almost certainly meaningless. In his turn, Montgomery gave her his office number.

'Ring me if you see or hear anything of Deborah,' he urged. 'You are our best lead for finding her. I don't think she'll be able to stay away from Henry for long.'

'If she comes, I'll stall her and let you know immediately,' promised Miss Goodridge. She accompanied him to the Metro, and it was a minute before they realized that Sergeant Bird wasn't there.

'He must have gone to inspect Henry again,' said Montgomery.

William Bird appeared a few seconds later looking unusually deferential. He had none of Jackson's misplaced arrogance, but one reason people enjoyed working with him was his avuncular air of confidence. He was the rock the whole department had leaned on at one time or another, yet just now he might have been a raw recruit tremblingly submitting to a senior officer a curriculum vitae he knew to be inadequate.

'Miss Goodridge,' he said gravely. 'I have a large Edwardian terraced house with a secluded back garden. My hours can be irregular, but not unduly so. I spend most of my evenings at home, reading and listening to music . . . ' Montgomery could scarcely contain his astonishment. For one ludicrous moment he thought that his widowed sergeant was offering a Collins-type proposal to this mature lady, then he heard the key words: 'Do you think that might be considered a suitable environment for Sam?'

'Hope he likes Bach,' muttered Montgomery gruffly.

Felicity Goodridge sent him a brief, amused smile before giving Sergeant Bird her full attention.

'It sounds ideal,' she said. 'Would there be a cat-flap? Elderly cats need access to facilities.'

'There would.'

'Excellent. What do you propose? I assume you're still on duty.'

'If it's acceptable to you, I'll return this evening, say at seven, with a stout box.'

'Until seven, then.'

Montgomery eyed his colleague as they jolted back down the track.

'William Bird, you're a big softie,' he said.

'I admit it. Luckily, so are a lot of others.' He wrenched the wheel round to avoid a particularly vicious pothole. 'Deborah, for instance. Suddenly I feel encouraged.'

'Yes.' Montgomery shared the sentiment, and not just because they had a promising lead. His heart had lightened for better reason than that: for the first time in the investigation, here was solid evidence that Deborah had left Thorbeck alive.

14

The sun was high and bright as Montgomery drove his own car along Venning Road. He passed the Health Centre, noting its overburdened car park, pulled up in the street beyond and walked back to the surgery entrance.

He needed to see Neville alone. That reference to Lynn in George's 'Evie' letter would practically guarantee non-cooperation if he called at Oaklands, yet Neville was the most likely person to know Evie's identity. There was something else Montgomery felt he knew, as well . . .

The glass-panelled door opened just as Montgomery was squeezing between two badly parked cars. Neville Wither-spoon himself stepped out, looked up at the sky with less appreciation than another man might have shown, and threaded his way stiffly towards the 'doctors only' portion of the car-park.

'Dr Witherspoon.'

Montgomery tried to make his call sound friendly and re-assuring, but Neville still jumped as if a firework had exploded at his heels. 'Inspector . . . Is there news of Deborah?'

'Some news, yes.' Montgomery was able to lower his voice as their paths converged. 'We've found Henry at a smallhold-ing out in the country, and a girl answering Deborah's de-scription took him there on Sunday morning.'

'Where?' Neville was instantly tense and animated, a mot-tled pink flush flaring across his cheeks. Montgomery knew what would happen if he divulged the information: Neville would storm up to Smilodon, interrogate Miss Goodridge and lurk in the area until Deborah had been thoroughly frightened off. With difficulty he persuaded the doctor that discretion was the best policy.

'But can't we have Henry home?' demanded Neville. 'Whoever is at the cat place could tell Deborah, and then we'd get her back again.'

Emotions could distort the simplest of truths, thought Montgomery. He spoke soothingly of 'neutral ground', and moved the subject away from Deborah before Neville could object.

'How is Martin?' he asked. 'Has he thrown any light on the reasons for his extraordinary confessions?'

'I'm afraid Martin has left home,' said Neville grimly. 'My wife thinks that's a good thing; I'm not so sure. He's gone to stay with Ray Cooper, one of the yobs from the building site.' Ostentatiously he looked at his watch.

'I see . . . well, I'd like to ask you something else if you can spare a minute. You may remember that there was a notepad among George's effects, which we took for forensic examination. It turned out that he had indeed written a recent letter and the recipient was a woman called Evie. What can you tell me about Evie?'

Neville's flush returned; he swung his gaze to the ground, and stared fixedly at the tarmac.

'I – nothing,' he mumbled. 'I've never heard the name.'

'I think you have. Who is she?'

'I've told you; I don't know. George had his own friends.'

'Dr Witherspoon, look at me. George wrote to Evie less than a week before his death. He rang someone – probably this woman – hours before he died. We think she may have come; she may have taken the spare key from behind the hose-pipe – yes, we know about that, so why shouldn't someone else? – let herself in through the kitchen door and murdered your brother. Don't you think you owe it to him to help us find her?'

'No . . . I mean, it could never have been like that. I don't believe it. There's no reason . . .'

'So you *do* know who she is.'

'No! What I meant was, there's no reason for anyone to have killed George. He was worn out; he couldn't have harmed a soul.'

'But he was killed, Dr Witherspoon. Our failure to rationalize it doesn't remove the fact.'

'You don't need to remind me of that. He was my brother, remember? If you're actually interested in my opinion, I'm convinced it was some wretched accident.'

'Like Maud?'

As soon as he had spoken the words, Montgomery felt ashamed of himself. Neville seemed to crumple, and for a brief space was pitiful, a hollow dummy of a man, a scarecrow form in smart clothes. Those ghastly dead bodies had been his closest relations . . .

Montgomery softened his tone, and decided to try for a different piece of information. Neville would disclose it, if only to get rid of his unwelcome interlocutor.

'The anonymous letters have stopped arriving,' he said, 'but we feel their author may have vital knowledge. So far, despite active measures, we haven't been able to track down this person. Have you any ideas at all?'

Neville blinked at him.

'The last time we discussed this question, I believe something occurred to you which you then dismissed, perhaps because you thought it was unlikely. I'd be grateful if you could share your idea, however silly it might seem. We're very short of leads.'

He could almost hear Neville's thought processes: give him this and he'll leave the other matter. Yes, vowed Montgomery, he would. Until next time.

'It was nothing solid, Inspector,' came the hesitant reply. 'Call it more of a notion, based on a look . . .'

'Would you care to explain?'

'Yes . . . well,' Neville squared his shoulders and assumed his dry professional persona, 'I have a patient who attends my surgery frequently. She has numerous vague symptoms, but neither I nor the hospital specialists have ever found any demonstrable pathology. Latterly, the focus of her complaints has been gynaecological. She – she, er, always wanted particularly to be seen by me, even when claiming a problem was urgent: I began to feel that this was an undesirable situation.' His face showed clearly how undesirable. 'A few weeks ago I transferred responsibility for her gynaecological difficulties to a clinic run by my colleague Dr Adams. The patient took this badly; in fact, she hasn't been back to me since.'

'Did she see Dr Adams?'

'Yes. Katherine confirms that there is nothing organically wrong with her.'

'Who is the patient, Dr Witherspoon?'

'Must I say?'

'Your mother is dead.'

'Yes . . . very well, then. She's called Harriet Lawson. I did wonder about her in connection with the letters; she garners all kinds of malicious titbits at the Ladies' Friendship Guild, and she was aware of the changes in Mother's will. But that didn't seem – enough, somehow, enough for the wicked allegations.'

'Let me be blunt. Do you think she hates you?'

Neville winced fastidiously. 'How can I answer that? Perhaps she does.'

As Neville left to make a domiciliary visit, Montgomery spotted a familiar figure behind the glass doors of the surgery. He spent time adjusting his windscreen wiper and waited for the person to emerge. Yes, it was Trudi Forester, resplendent in a purple Liberty outfit. She turned his way without hesitation.

'Inspector Montgomery – hello. I didn't want to interrupt you with poor Neville just now, but it's nice to see you again. Were you hoping to interview Kenneth?'

'Not on this occasion.'

'Oh, that's lucky. He's on the telephone, trying to get hold of an important lab result, and the hospital keep cutting him off. He's getting quite irate. We were going to go for lunch later, but now he's got too much work. I don't suppose *you*'d be free for lunch with a lady, would you?' She undermined her charm by standing six inches too close to him, violating Montgomery's sense of personal space.

'No time, I'm afraid,' he said; the obvious riposte was too cruel.

122

'What a pity. I must confess I'm *dying* to know how your enquiry is progressing. I'm sure I could help you. I know all about the surgery and how it works. I know Neville and his family . . . ' She gave a light chuckle. 'He's a funny old thing. Dry and worthy in most people's estimations, a really dull dog – yet he must have had a spark of life in his youth: did anyone tell you he jilted his first fiancée? No – I imagine you won't get much background from other people because they all have something to hide. But I've got no axe to grind. Come round for a drink some afternoon – make it soon.'

God save me from bored housewives, thought Montgomery, feeling a sudden strong dislike for Trudi Forester. How badly she was overplaying her hand! Yet despite his instinctive personal disgust, the policeman's portion of his mind, necessarily dispassionate, was enlarging on its former assessment of Kenneth Forester's wife, and raising an interesting observation: if the letter-writer was a woman, in or close to her forties, who was conversant with Neville's affairs, then it wasn't only Harriet Lawson who fitted the bill.

He forced himself to smile. 'Thank you; perhaps I might manage that.'

In Thorbeck's village hall, Carole Montgomery steeled herself to catch Harriet Lawson's eye. 'Try to get her on to the subject of doctors,' Richard had said, having effortlessly transferred his attentions from Gertrude Weddell Grant to Harriet. 'Then see if you can acquire a sample of her writing.' Simple!(?)

By her side, Joan was keeping up a muted commentary.

'Careful, Carole, Harriet's looking this way. You don't want to get involved with *her*; all she's interested in is picking up gossip to pass on to someone else. Oh heavens, she's coming over. I think it's you she wants to talk to. Whatever you do, don't let her start on the subject of doctors or you'll be landed for the next hour . . . '

Within five minutes Carole and Harriet were discussing tension headaches, and Joan had slunk away for a sausage roll.

'. . . It's not the sort of thing I'd want to trouble my doctor with, though,' Carole murmured.

'Doctors!' Harriet made a scathing sound. 'They don't care. They're not really interested in their patients; they just want to scribble a prescription and get you out of their surgery as quickly as possible.'

'Mine isn't like that.'

'Let me tell you, I could have a serious illness, but they won't find out until it's too late.' Unprompted, she delivered a verbal pageant of specific details, finishing with another broadside against her GP. 'Dr Witherspoon isn't competent to deal with women's problems,' she said, 'so he's washed his hands of me and passed me on to one of his partners, Dr Adams. Without a "by your leave". She's not *my* idea of a doctor. Brusque, unsympathetic . . . women like her shouldn't be dealing with patients. I ought to have been sent to another specialist in any case.'

Carole maintained a blandly receptive expression with difficulty. Katherine Adams was her own GP, and in her estimation was kind, proficient and easy to talk to. Perhaps Harriet resented being given the same limited appointment time as everybody else.

Joan appeared suddenly behind Harriet's shoulder. 'Mrs Tye would like to see you about your membership subscription,' she said to Carole, accompanying her words with a broad wink.

'In a minute, thanks, Joan.'

'But she has the book out.' Joan tilted her head towards Harriet and raised her eyebrows.

'I won't be long.'

As her friend flushed with annoyance and turned away, Carole applied her mind to the problem of obtaining a sample of Harriet's writing. Her initial plan, that of clandestinely acquiring Harriet's diary, she had abandoned in a hot flurry of belated guilt. Such an action would be tantamount to petty larceny. Even knocking the book out of its owner's hand, substituting another and rushing off to the Ladies Room with tracing paper held a taint of underhandedness, and effecting the return swap would present insuperable problems.

With a mental sigh, she looked round for inspiration. The

evening was practically over, and the ladies were milling about informally holding their diverse conversations. There was Gertrude Weddell Grant, leaning over a table to sign some sort of card. She wore a large-patterned dress in her usual bold colours, but when she raised her head Carole was shocked: above the heavy jowls Gertrude's face was haunted. Her eyes flickered suspiciously over the groups of her companions, alighting on one, narrowing a little and moving away again, and her knuckles, with all their garish rings, were clenched.

Harriet was still droning on, and Carole interjected a tactical 'My goodness!' before continuing her covert surveillance. Now Gertrude was forcing her way through the crowd, apparently *en route* to the Guild's president. Her path took her close to Harriet, whom she totally ignored; Harriet, for her part, flashed her a look of strange, bitter triumph.

Before Carole could puzzle over this display, the president called the assembly to order.

'Ladies, there's one final point before we all go home,' she said. 'Miss Rattigan is still ill with flu, so we're signing a card for her tonight. Please be sure to put your name down; thank you.'

Minutes later, Joan appeared with Mrs Tye.

'Do you know Miss Rattigan?' the treasurer asked Carole.

'Yes; I met her here a month ago.'

'Then you must sign the card. I think that's everyone.'

As she placed the card on a nearby table, Carole noticed the address on the unstamped envelope.

'I live near there,' she said brightly, stretching truth to its broadest limits. 'I can deliver it if you like.'

'Oh – that would be nice of you.'

Carole took a pen from her handbag and added her name to the right-hand column of signatures: just above it, an expansively scrawled 'Gertrude' took up room for three, but the real prize skulked toad-like in the centre of the column opposite: thirteen cramped letters from the niggardly hand of Harriet Lawson.

*

125

Jackson and Smythe tramped along a narrow street running behind Nottingham's main bus station, and discussed Deborah. Their search for her had so far met with silence and blank stares, but Montgomery seemed to think that Hope in the City might offer a springboard for fruitful enquiries.

'Deborah doesn't sound like the kind of girl who'd be able to live rough,' said Smythe as they checked the doors of each tall building.

Jackson eyed his companion with a wry smile; Smythe might have been talking about himself. He was the least macho of all the detective constables, with his quiet voice and lustrous brown eyes. For a while he had adopted an extreme form of crew cut in an attempt to vitiate his poetic features, but realizing that no one was fooled he had allowed the dark hair to grow again; Jackson suspected that Smythe's mother had had more than a nominal hand in the decision.

'It might not be a question of choice if her money's run out,' he replied. 'The boss is sure she'll stay in this general area because of the cat; these charity people will know all the main dossing-down spots.'

'Fifty-seven B,' read Smythe, halting outside a grimy brick building which housed the offices of a tea company on its first two floors. In the second floor windows they could see posters depicting shabbily dressed teenagers slumped in various attitudes of despair above a gaudy telephone number.

'Well, if it isn't the Samaritans, we've got the right place,' said Jackson, and thrust his way forward to take charge.

At the top of two flights of wooden stairs, a door announced HOPE IN THE CITY; they knocked, entered and found a small untidy office manned by two young people. The nearest, a boy of about twenty-two, had an earring in his right ear and an intelligent face.

'Hello?' he said, not quite able to place his visitors or guess their business.

'Police,' said Jackson, producing his warrant card.

The boy's face sagged in dismay.

'Oh, hell,' he groaned. 'Who called *you* in?'

15

'It's fraud.' Jackson faced Montgomery squarely and tried to keep the note of triumph out of his voice; bombast was high on the inspector's list of *bêtes noires*.

His tone found a more confidential level. 'Our Mrs Weddell Grant has been siphoning off charity funds,' he said. 'The staff of Hope in the City have harboured suspicions for some time, but couldn't find a decent excuse to look at the books. They suggested to Mrs Weddell Grant that it might be considered unusual in some quarters for the treasurer of a charity to be on the committee of one of their main donor organizations, but she laughed it off, saying it meant she could jolly people into giving more. After some thought they came up with a better idea: they proposed that no treasurer should serve for more than two years. The proposal was adopted.'

'She's almost at the end of her tenure,' put in Smythe. 'She had to hand over the accounts so that the next treasurer could familiarize herself with the system . . . but they're now being audited. The accountants believe several of the entries are false.'

'You said they weren't pleased to see you,' commented Montgomery.

'That's right.' Jackson resumed the tale. 'They wanted to sort it out internally if possible, but when we turned up the silly sods thought someone had blown the gaff. One of the girls who works there is Harriet Lawson's niece, you see, so they reckoned she was responsible. They told us everything.'

'How long do they think Gertrude has been embezzling their money?'

127

'As treasurer, probably the full two years, but before that she was a general fund-raiser and they admit their accounts were sloppily kept. I would bet she's been at it for as long as her involvement with charity work.'

'Do the dates tie in with Maud Witherspoon in any way?'

'They do. Maud Witherspoon died at just the time Gertrude needed hard cash to replace the amounts she'd taken. She would have known at that point that a new treasurer was due to be elected, but thought she had a month or two's grace before anyone started asking for the accounts. She was wrong, hence the hasty falsifications. We can safely assume she didn't find the money.'

'It fits, sir,' insisted Smythe enthusiastically. 'We know Mrs Weddell Grant went to see Mrs Witherspoon just before the rumours about the proposed new will started up. It was probably her suggestion! She visited twice more, and the second time was only two days before the old lady died – you told us that. She must have thought the altered will was valid, and she could adjust the documentation of the charity bequest to cover the missing sums.'

'Hmm.' Montgomery was thoughtful. 'What's your theory about the warfarin? It would have been the height of ineptitude to kill Maud just *before* the will was due to be changed.'

'I visualize it like this, sir.' Smythe's face glowed with zeal. 'Mrs Weddell Grant visits Oaklands and sits with Mrs Witherspoon. When the old lady has either nodded off or become distracted with a drink or a gift, Gertrude slips the warfarin into a bottle of legitimate pills, making sure it goes near the bottom so there's no danger of it being taken too soon.'

'What colour are warfarin tablets?' asked Sergeant Bird.

'I – I don't know,' faltered Smythe.

'Neither do I,' said Montgomery, 'but Gertrude would be lucky to find that they just matched the tablets she was mixing them with. It sounds risky to me – too much fumbling about. From what we've been told, Maud was a sharp woman, unlikely to doze in the presence of someone like Gertrude. Still, Graham, you could be right . . . except that we've nothing to tie Gertrude in with George. *His* will didn't favour the charity.'

'Perhaps he discovered something incriminating.'

'Which is more than we can manage. Well done so far, you two, but we need more. Until definitive evidence of fraud is unearthed, I suggest we avoid tackling Mrs Weddell Grant herself. Try to find out by indirect means whether she took Maud a box of chocolates or something. Think where she might have obtained access to warfarin. Find out if she knew George . . .

'In the meantime, I consider that the "Evie" letter is too damning to ignore, so Will and I will make it our business to unmask this woman.'

'Be useful if it turned out to be Gertrude,' grinned Jackson.

'Stranger things have been known.'

Sergeant Bird returned from a sortie in the middle of the afternoon, and headed gratefully to the canteen with Montgomery.

'Nothing from George's erstwhile landlady in Radford,' he said, biting into a huge pastry. He chewed, swallowed and sighed appreciatively. 'These are good, you know. Why don't you try one yourself?'

'Nothing at all?' asked Montgomery, ignoring the talk of food. It was rare for him to eat between meals.

'I'm afraid not. She remembered him well enough, because he'd lived there for four years, but she couldn't describe a single friend of his. The name Evie rang no bells. She claimed that women weren't welcome there anyway, because both her tenants had been single men and she "liked to keep a respectable house". You should have seen it, sir: a decaying wreck run by a slattern; respectable it wasn't. One could certainly understand why George snapped up his brother's offer of a home.'

'I thought landladies were irretrievably nosy. Didn't she post letters for him, or peer at his incoming mail?'

'I gather most of his correspondence was the buff-envelope

type – bills, not dirty books. And anyway, George only recently became too immobile to do his own errands.' He leaned forward. 'You know, sir, I've got a hunch about this Evie letter. There's a flavour of the past about it, as if he's trying to revive a relationship which died or failed to flourish years ago. Something about that "ever yours", and the references to Neville and Lynn. We assumed she'd visited the flat and been disgusted by it, but that might not be the case. He could have been saying: "I didn't invite you before, because my flat wasn't worthy of you, but now my situation is better I'd love to see you."'

'You think the move to Neville's was the trigger, then?'

'Either that, or he'd heard of some change in Evie's circumstances which encouraged him. Perhaps her partner had disappeared from the scene.'

Evie . . . Montgomery contemplated the name while William Bird munched his pastry. To him, it held shades of exotic untouchability, like a tropical bird of exceptional beauty roosting just out of reach. There had been reverence in George's letter, and supplication – and yet . . . Montgomery gave a small click of self-derision; he had no real basis for these ideas. 'Evie girl' sounded familiar enough: she was probably just some tart after all, a casual pick-up George had woven dreams around, fantasies to stave off his loneliness . . .

Montgomery looked sharply at William Bird. 'How's Sam?' he asked.

'Oh, settling in nicely, thanks. We're still getting to know each other, but mutual respect is growing. There's just one problem – he's taken a fancy to my best chair.'

Montgomery smiled. From what he had heard of cats, that would be 'Sam's chair' within a week. He drained his cup.

'I've got two suggestions for tracking down Evie,' he said. 'The first is Mr Barton, who has been solicitor to both Witherspoon brothers. We know that the bulk of George's estate is earmarked for his nephew and niece, but there might be an individual bequest for Evie, which would give her full name. Would you check up on that? The other possible avenue is Angela Cording. She was Neville's next-door neighbour for

130

several years. Perhaps she knew George; maybe he introduced her to Evie. I think the chances are reasonable.'

Sergeant Bird was puzzled. 'Surely it would be more direct to ask Neville himself?'

'I have done. He knows all right – but he's not telling.'

Angela Cording's settee was surrounded by papers. 'I'm sorry about the mess,' she said. 'I'm just finishing my article for next month's issue. Deadlines are a mixed blessing, you know; on the one hand they can make you feel like a machine, but on the other – boy, are they a spur to get things done! Here's a seat for you; do sit down.'

'I won't bother you for long,' said Montgomery, perching on a hard dining chair after almost treading on Minou. 'I came to ask if you ever met Dr Witherspoon's brother George.'

A broad smile caused Angela's face to crinkle attractively. 'George!' she exclaimed with reminiscent warmth. 'He was always the court jester when he came to visit Neville. The stuffier Neville got, the more George played up.'

'You knew him fairly well?'

'Yes. He went out fishing with Peter two or three times. He had nicknames for both of us: mine was "Shortie", would you believe?' Yes, thought Montgomery. She stood an estimated five feet ten in stockinged feet. 'I'm ashamed to say that we lost touch with George after Neville moved from the district. But I heard recently that his health was failing, and I keep meaning to find out where he's living now and drop him a line.'

Gently Montgomery appraised her of the bad news, and saw genuine regret in her face.

'What a pity,' she said. 'He can't have been any age . . . Still, I know he took what he could from life while he had the chance.'

'Did you ever meet any of his lady friends?'

'No – I suppose they're scattered in ports all around the world.'

'Are you sure? Was there anyone local called Eve, or Evie?'

131

She thought for a moment, then shook her head. 'I'm sorry.'

'Nobody of that name connected with Neville or Lynn?'

'Truly – it doesn't sound at all familiar.'

'Never mind.'

The hunt was becoming frustrating. Irrationally, Montgomery had had high hopes of Angela Cording, but it wasn't her fault if those hopes were not fulfilled. He felt that William was right, that 'Evie' was an echo from George's past, and only contemporaries from a certain era could provide clues to her identity. Who else might know? Neville was keeping quiet, his parents were dead, his wife was hostile and his children were too young.

As Montgomery drove back towards the station, he saw a blonde-haired woman on the pavement whose undulating gait reminded him of Trudi Forester. He slowed down, knowing he should call on Trudi, reluctant to tangle with her again so soon. Professionalism won; minutes later, he was speeding away from a telephone box, taking the road which led to the Foresters' home.

'George? No, I never did meet him. I heard he was *unpresentable.*' Trudi Forester raised her eyebrows and chuckled conspiratorially at Montgomery. Once again she had offered him the sofa, and this time settled herself at the other end, smoothing her skirt over her elegant knees with a practised movement.

'In what way?' asked Montgomery.

'His general lifestyle – surely you know. Women, drink, brawls – the lot. I gather he delighted in doing everything Neville abhorred. I suppose psychologists would say he was rebelling against his upbringing, much as Martin is doing now. I knew old Maud Witherspoon slightly, and she was enough to make anyone rebel.'

'Did you ever hear mention of any of George's girl friends?'

She grinned. 'There was one – Foochow Flora. You don't forget a name like that.'

'Nobody in England?'

'Sorry, I don't know.'

'Did the name "Evie" ever crop up in conjunction with George?'

'Evie . . . ? No.'

'What about Neville? Does he have an acquaintance called Eve or Evie?'

'Not one I've met – but I can try to find out for you. Is it important?' Trudi leaned towards him, her curiosity almost palpable, stifling as sweat. There was a malachite glitter in her eyes and her well-glossed lips hung slightly apart, revealing her lower teeth.

'Possibly.' Montgomery made his voice deliberately dismissive. Much as he needed hard evidence to help him solve the case, he didn't want Trudi Forester ferreting around on his behalf. There had to be other ways.

Trudi was waiting, watching him, craving involvement. To defuse her eagerness, Montgomery made a casual enquiry about the proposed changes to the practice once Bernard Quested retired. Under cover of her detailed monologue he thought hard. There was one more possibility: Neville's jilted fiancée, whoever she was, might have met Evie with George.

'. . . so Ken's responsibilities will be as major as Neville's,' Trudi was saying. 'It's only right; he has solid experience of general practice. Someone asked me once why Ken's name was above Katherine's on the plate, even though he's seven years younger. I told her in no uncertain terms that Ken was there first, and Katherine had wasted years in hospital medicine, doing some dreary clinical assistant job. No, Ken will be running the practice one day.' She pronounced this sentence like a mantra, and Montgomery had a sudden image of her hissing the words at her dressing-table mirror every morning. If it wasn't for the fact that Harriet Lawson was almost certainly their anonymous correspondent he would be on the alert for a piece of Trudi's handwriting.

'I hope our investigation hasn't upset Dr Witherspoon's

133

patients,' he said. There had been a splurge of grisly publicity in the local media following the exhumation of Maud.

'No ... I don't think it has.' She sounded rather non-plussed. 'However, if Neville personally should end up in serious trouble,' she flicked a probing glance at Montgomery, 'that would, of course, be different.'

She really dislikes him, thought Montgomery. She sees him as a barrier to the progress of that lightweight husband of hers. How ridiculous other people's aspirations could appear – yet a police officer ignored such things at his or her peril.

'How is Lynn managing?' he asked. 'Do you see anything of her?'

Trudi's mouth drooped. 'Just because our husbands work together, Inspector, it doesn't mean the wives live in each other's pockets. I told you before that Lynn is dour. She's also socially incompetent, and has at least enough savvy to know that she wouldn't fit in with my set. So I'm sorry – no woman-to-woman chats to report.'

'She seems an odd choice of wife for an established family doctor to make,' murmured Montgomery.

Trudi's urbane façade cracked completely. 'You could say they deserve each other,' she sneered. 'Neville's hardly normal ... But in any case he wasn't after looks, brains or a *cordon bleu* diploma; he simply wanted a brood mare. Katherine had insisted on putting her career before children; it's a pity she went on to make such a poor choice of husband herself.'

Montgomery's hands were suddenly icy. 'Katherine?' he repeated.

'Yes – Katherine Adams. She was engaged to Neville years ago, when they were both working at the Victoria Hospital. Then Neville went into general practice and set his heart on having a family. Katherine wanted to wait; within three months she was out in the cold and he'd married a clerk.' She shrugged. 'That's the way it goes, isn't it?'

Montgomery was aware of his own increased respiratory rate; he wanted to be out of that house, out in clean air, away from Trudi Forester, her lasciviousness and pretension, her

134

insensitivity and her spite. But he had to find out just a little more . . .

'Isn't it difficult for them, now that they work together in the same practice?' he asked idly.

Trudi made a careless gesture. 'The option was theirs. Passion must have long since died – if there ever was any. But I'm sure that's why Lynn never goes to Venning Road; she's still so insecure she doesn't want to run across Neville's first refusal.'

'Even though Katherine herself has been married in the meantime?'

'Oh, Herman never counted for much. He was a compulsive gambler. Their divorce only became absolute recently, but they've been separated for years.'

'Is Adams her married name?'

'No, her maiden name; she kept it for professional reasons.' Trudi stretched with feline grace, wriggled a little closer and gave Montgomery a teasing look. 'If you're going to ask questions all afternoon, Inspector, can I persuade you to join me in a drink? I've got – where are you going?'

Montgomery had risen from the depths of the settee in one decisive movement.

'I must continue my enquiries,' he said. 'Thank you for your help. Please don't worry about seeing me out.'

But she did, and behind a fixed smile her face was cheated and hostile, just the countenance Harriet Lawson must have worn when dismissed by Neville. Montgomery walked through the hall unabashed. He saw a bookcase there, filled with reference books of Kenneth's: medicine and pharmacology for when he was called at home. He noticed, too, some unopened mail, one letter addressed to Mrs T. E. Forester. It didn't matter; none of it did. He already knew who Evie was.

Katherine Adams's home was as immaculate and individual as her looks. It was part of a white Georgian terrace which stood in a quiet area of the city centre between the castle and the Playhouse. Inside were polished floors, Chinese rugs and pastel walls which gave pale prominence to framed watercolours and pen-and-ink sketches, all originals by little-known artists.

Montgomery appreciated the lack of clutter; it struck a chord of empathy in his soul. But he was not there to be empathetic. He put his question firmly.

'George called you "Evie", didn't he?'

'That's right. I wonder who told you. Was it Neville?'

'No.' Angela Cording had told him, although he hadn't realized it at the time. Nicknames for George's friends, using the obvious expedient of opposites ... no subtlety about George.

He stared at Katherine's fine features.

'How can I help you, Inspector Montgomery?'

'Tell me about your relationship with George.'

She spread her slender, capable hands. 'There wasn't one. Nothing more than friendship, that is. I met George through Neville, to whom I was once briefly engaged, but didn't see much of him until after the engagement was dissolved. He came home from the Merchant Navy for a long leave, and we spent some time together, just in a friendly way. I didn't want any kind of commitment, and thought that George felt the same. Then one evening he – declared himself. I was surprised by his intensity. The fun had to stop there and then; I had no intention of using him for my entertainment. He went back to sea; we exchanged odd postcards and Christmas greetings ... then the correspondence lapsed.

'Doubtless George heard about my marriage to Herman from Neville; similarly he knew when we were finally divorced last year. Just a few weeks ago he telephoned me here, and invited me to his flat. I had reservations: his tone was too vehement – he used expressions like "I've waited so long" – and I thought it would be cruel to mislead him by accepting. I spoke of workloads, meetings and Bernard's retirement, and managed to evade the specific issue. In the back of my mind I thought it might be possible to see him at some future date in an unsuggestive group setting, perhaps with Neville.

'Unfortunately, that wasn't the end of it. He wrote to me from Oaklands, pretending to have misunderstood by denigrating his flat. He then telephoned again, but I hardly had a chance to say anything because he rang off abruptly: I think someone must have come within earshot, Lynn perhaps. George was asking me to come to Oaklands while the family were out. I would have said no. As it is, I now know he had a fatal asthma attack that day, and I might have been able to help him. I regret the fact that I didn't.'

She raised her eyes to his; they were a lustrous brown with large pupils. *Belladonna*, thought Montgomery wryly ... Aileen's cats.

He wanted to challenge her, get it over with, but if he did, he knew he would never hear the rest.

'Neville and George were very unlike in personality,' he said, 'yet you had a relationship of sorts with each of them. How was that?'

Katherine Adams smiled. 'Attractions aren't mutually exclusive,' she said. 'We'd have no circles of friends if that was the case. No, we look for different things in different people. When I was twenty-four, I admired Neville for his brains and sense of purpose; he was four years older than I, and it was easy to imagine myself in love with him for a time. He was respectable, he was *suitable*, and although he lacked humour, there was no sign then of bigotry and dogmatism. I now know we would have been very unhappy together ... George, on the other hand, was fun, with his *risqué* jokes and ill-devised junkets; he was like a naughty brother, emotionally undemanding, until his attitude changed. I knew he was feckless, unreliable and certain to underachieve ... I would never have tied myself to George.'

'Yet you went on to marry a man with similar tendencies,' observed Montgomery.

'That's not true. George I could read right from the start; Herman's weaknesses were latent when I first knew him. He was a middle manager with East Midlands Boilers, and quite a stable individual until he was unexpectedly made redundant. Then he started gambling ... ' Her eyes darkened, the pupils dilating even more with her first sign of anger. 'He found that casino on the outskirts of Broxtowe – it was new in those days. Once he'd been in there, he was hooked. I was a medical registrar at the Victoria, working to keep a roof over our heads, while he was losing money at a frightening rate in that God-forsaken place. Sometimes he'd get despondent and swear to give it up, but then he'd make a small win and he'd be back at the roulette wheel or the pontoon table. There were women there, too, who would flatter him if he was doing well, making him feel big. I know he had affairs ... he did get another job, but lost it after two months.'

She looked at Montgomery frankly. 'I'm sure you don't need all the details; the tale's a familiar one. Broken promises, scenes, degradation, despair. For a while he went to Gamblers' Anonymous, and I tried to give him some stability by taking up a clinical assistant post at the hospital, which offered an open-ended contract. I couldn't be whole-hearted about my career while we were in such crisis: that kind of post is a side-step from the real career ladder, a cul-de-sac; you're a dogsbody with no authority and no real prospects. And in the end it was for nothing, because I couldn't save him.'

Her gaze fell away from Montgomery's. 'I didn't love him any more. He didn't want help from me or any organization. In fact he blamed me, said I made him feel inadequate. We separated. He lives in Derby now with some woman who thinks she can change him.'

'And you moved into general practice.'

'Yes.'

There was silence. Her story was no doubt true, but its dispassionate delivery conspired to mislead. Years of medical training, of resisting the emotional assault of often desperate patients, had forged a jacket of steel around Katherine Adams's spontaneity, and Montgomery could only guess what lay behind. How did she really regard Neville, who, if Sister Tarrant was to be believed, was treating her badly all over again? Were the old hidden wounds gaping, sharp and raw? He wished he knew.

'May I see George's letter?' he asked slowly.

'I – no; I'm sorry – I threw it away.'

'You're sure?'

'Yes.'

He paused. 'Would you kindly outline for me your movements on the afternoon he died? That was Saturday, July the eighth.'

The change in her manner was scarcely perceptible, but Montgomery had been watching for it. In a breath, whatever impersonal brand of goodwill she had been offering him was withdrawn.

'The day Deborah went missing,' she said. 'Yes; I was shopping in town.'

'Was anyone with you?'

'No. I always consider that a recipe for disaster.'

'Do you have any till receipts or credit card slips to record your purchases?'

'It's unlikely; I was window-shopping and buying groceries; I often pay cash, but even if I used my switch card, the entry would appear on my bank statement several days too late.'

'What about the supermarket till receipt?'

'I discard them when I reach home.'

Everything tidy, everything dealt with . . . Did that include George?

Katherine Adams was speaking again:

'Kenneth hinted to me that there were unusual features surrounding George's death,' she said. 'Evidently you think so too, even though the cause turned out to be asthma. Can I assure you I had nothing to do with it, and never even saw him that day?'

'I note your comment,' said Montgomery.

She stood up. 'I see. Well, it's almost time for evening surgery. I'll make my preparations, if it's all right with you.'

He nodded solemnly and followed her into the pale green hall. A watercolour painting near the door depicted an autumn hedgerow scene: Dr Adams recognized his interest.

'That was from one of my patients.'

'Ah; I noticed you had a Roskell original in the sitting-room. They're beginning to appreciate now, according to the Sunday supplements.'

She gave an ironic smile, her hand on the door-knob. 'You think they're my investment portfolio? I'm afraid you're wrong. I buy paintings because I like them, and I can come home these days without wondering if they've been sold while I was out. I'm shaping my own life now, Inspector – the way I want it.'

Had that been a challenge, Montgomery reflected as he threaded through the late afternoon traffic *en route* to the station. He had ambivalent feelings about the interview. Katherine Adams the woman he had scarcely been allowed to glimpse, and for this he was more sorry than he cared to acknowledge. Yet Katherine Adams the doctor remained a prime suspect for the murders as far as circumstantial evidence was concerned. True, she had freely confessed to being 'Evie', but arguably lying would have been too dangerous. She had ample access to warfarin and to records of Maud Witherspoon's medications; it would have been child's play to tamper with a bottle of pills prepared for Maud in the practice dispensary, a bottle then carried to the patient by an unwitting Bernard Quested – or even Neville himself. That damning letter sufficed for the death of George.

Carole's GP, he thought belatedly as he swung into the station car-park. Katherine had mentioned only part of the truth: not only do we look for different things in different people, we *are* different things to different people. Imagine the clutch of testimonials if it ever came to trial – striving to balance one flimsy but incriminating letter which she might yet deny ever having received. Montgomery sighed; their next meeting could well be an even more frigid catechism under the solemn shadow of an official caution . . .

He climbed out of his Sierra and headed for the door to the back stairs which led to the CID floor. Before he could reach it, a uniformed constable rounded the corner of the building, waved, and called to him.

'Sir – glad you're back. Constable Jenkins wants a word with you urgently; he's on the switchboard.'

Montgomery hurried to the main public entrance, circumnavigated the desk and waited until Jenkins had finished advising a woman about her lost dog.

140

'Sir!' He looked up at Montgomery, his face glowing pink with an amalgam of eagerness and anxiety. 'A call came through here fifteen minutes ago. It was a young girl, very tearful and upset. She said her name was Deborah – and she can't come home because she's killed her grandmother!'

16

Montgomery received the news with a sick twist in his gut. Taken at face value, it confirmed his original instinct that the Witherspoon affair was a family matter, even down to the use of their pet. And yet . . . if the caller *hadn't* been Deborah, how cynical and callous was their adversary!

'Was it a 999?' he demanded.

'No, sir; just an ordinary line.'

Damn; there would be no recording. 'What time exactly?'

'Seventeen minutes past four.' Less than ten minutes from the time he had left Katherine Adams . . .

Montgomery waved Jenkins back to his seat and pulled up a nearby chair for himself.

'Think carefully,' he urged. 'Are you positive it was a young girl? Could it have been a woman trying to *sound* like a young girl?'

'No.' He shook his head vigorously. 'Her voice was thin and high, just like a teenager. She was genuinely upset, too, gulping back tears.'

'What exactly did she say?'

'Well, nothing at first. I'd said "Nottinghamshire Police, can I help you?" and there was just this faint snuffling, so I said "Hello?" and she said "Is that the police?" and I said "Yes, what can I do for you?" Then there was another long pause before she said in a sort of quivering gasp: "My name is Deborah . . . Tell them not to look for me, because I can't come home. I killed my grandmother!" Then she burst into tears, and just as I was about to ask her where she was, she hung up. Do you think it's Deborah Witherspoon, the missing girl, sir?'

'I don't know.' Montgomery was torn by indecision. Was it a cruel hoax from some shabby subhuman? He had encountered enough of those in his time. Or was it Deborah herself, distraught and possibly suicidal? Despite sweeping efforts, they were no closer to finding her.

'It could well be,' he added, standing once more as new calls registered on the switchboard. 'Let me know immediately if she rings back. I'll be upstairs for the next hour or so.'

He left Jenkins and made his way to the CID floor. He would get the call traced, of course, but the odds favoured an unremarkable phone box in the city centre. So what now? He must breathe fresh life into his team, organize yet more publicity – and pray that they find Deborah in time.

'Your radio appeal last night did the trick, sir,' said Colin Haslam the next day.

'Go on,' said Montgomery. The other officers crowded round the burly detective constable, keen to hear something hopeful.

'A Mrs Miller rang in. She runs a bed-and-breakfast business from the family farmhouse out near Awsworth. Apparently a girl answering Deborah's general description stayed two nights with her: Saturday the eighth and Sunday the ninth. The girl looked about twenty, and claimed to have come to the district for a job interview on the Monday morning. She was out most of Sunday – said she'd been visiting friends.'

'What about the cat?'

'There was no cat with her, sir, neither was one mentioned. But there is something else: she both arrived and left in a taxi. We started working through the firms again, and a driver does remember collecting her from the farm. He took her to the city centre – Trinity Square, to be precise.'

'The bus station,' murmured Sergeant Bird.

'Well done, Colin. Has anyone checked with the building society people to see if she's attempted to withdraw any cash?'

'Yes,' said Grange, Haslam's equally rugged partner.

'She hasn't. She probably guesses we've alerted the staff there.'

Montgomery nodded his agreement. 'For those who haven't heard, Documents have confirmed that Harriet Lawson's writing matches that on the anonymous letters, even though the hand was disguised. I'm not interested in her petty grievances but if she actually knows something useful, that will be a different matter. Will and I will confront her this afternoon, but right now I want to take stock: we've got two murders here, and various pointers towards individuals who may be guilty, but nothing more concrete. We can't let these other issues side-track us completely.

'Looking first at the Witherspoon family, we have to ask ourselves: what motives and opportunities might each member have had? Neville had the necessary access to drugs but nothing to gain, as far as I can see, from using them. He's lost his mother and brother, and become the butt of village scandal. His wider reputation as a GP may yet suffer. We might conclude, then, that our killer has it in for Neville. I believe Neville himself is innocent.

'Lynn Witherspoon I find hard to assess. She's a drab woman with a sullen, put-upon air, possibly a consequence of years of ministering to the old lady, and latterly to her brother-in-law George. If she's our killer, the motive lies in the arena of emotions rather than finance.'

'Unless she was protecting the children's interests,' chipped in Jackson.

'Point taken. That would mean that she, at least, believed the rumours and judged Maud capable of disinheriting them. So what about opportunity? Perfect for poisoning Maud, although the source of the warfarin is less clear. But she was out with Neville for the whole of the afternoon of George's death. They went to Hardwick Hall.'

'Sir . . . ' Smythe raised his hand a few diffident inches.

'Yes, Graham?'

'I was wondering . . . are we so sure that George's death was murder? If he just happened to die that afternoon because the cat got in by accident, then we're only looking at Maud's death, and Lynn isn't excluded.'

'I went through that with Neville,' replied Montgomery. 'Henry couldn't have reached the dining-room by accident. The crux of the matter is the catmint. It was stuffed in George's pocket in order to keep Henry on his lap; that spells murder to me.'

Smythe subsided, and Montgomery continued: 'Next there's Martin, the son by adoption. He's an odd boy who confesses to murders and hides good deeds from his family. If he *is* guilty after all, and he's killed for money, then he picked a very strange time to dispatch Maud. He had little opportunity in any case, and none at all for George. If his aim was to stem the destructive effect of these two invalids on family life, then we must face the fact that such a motive is even more applicable to the people actually burdened with the drudgery: Lynn and Deborah.'

He paused, experiencing the now-familiar unease at the mention of Deborah's name. Could a fifteen-year-old be guilty of such things? Were they to encounter that bleakest of tableaux at the culmination of their search – the discovery of a young girl's lifeless body? Maybe even now Deborah was cramming warfarin into her mouth, tablets from her own father's surgery . . .

'So we come to Deborah herself,' he said briskly. 'She had motive and opportunity for both killings if we assume she sneaked back to the house on the Saturday afternoon when her parents had left.' He frowned. 'We didn't ask Aileen when Deborah actually arrived; at the time we were more interested in her journey home. That omission should be remedied. Another factor is her relationship with Henry: the cat would be pliant with her, less so with others.'

'I have to confess, I can't envisage George being so "pliant",' interjected Sergeant Bird. 'Wouldn't he sweep the cat off his knee, rather than lie there being suffocated by asthma?'

'He was probably asleep at first. Imagine it – lunch, a comfortable chair and no one around to interrupt him. Even though he was sitting in the window hoping Katherine Adams would call, it was a warm day and he was likely to doze. The killer would then sneak in and keep Henry close to

George, but not touching him. Perhaps the cat was stroked to make his fur fly into the air. I've seen people who are acutely allergic to cats: within minutes their eyes and noses are streaming. In George's case, his lungs seized up. He was very likely *in extremis* by the time our killer tucked catmint in his pockets and plonked Henry on his lap.'

'Ugh,' said Grange with feeling.

'So that's the position of the Witherspoons,' continued Montgomery. 'There are three outsiders we should also consider. Harriet Lawson ought to be mentioned, but I think we can rule her out as the actual murderer: when Maud died, Harriet hadn't been near Oaklands for a month.

'Gertrude Weddell Grant had a strong financial motive for killing the old lady: Brian and Graham have provided us with that. We haven't pinpointed the method used, though; she visited on the Wednesday and only brought a pot-plant. I still feel it was risky if she doctored something of Maud's on that visit – Maud might have died *before* the will was revised. There's nothing to link Gertrude with George, either.

'Finally, we've got Katherine Adams . . . ' He had already shared with them his 'Evie' revelations; now he dissected Katherine's past life and present situation in trenchant sentences, aware of the kindly but sagacious eye of Sergeant Bird.

'She had medical knowledge,' he finished up, 'drugs to hand – and a barn-door opportunity for killing George. Only the motive is obscure, but hatred for Neville could well be at the core of it.'

'There's one more element,' said Sergeant Bird reluctantly. 'I made enquiries about George's will, which he only made a few months ago when his health began deteriorating in earnest: he left seventy-five per cent of his estate jointly to his nephew and niece, and the other twenty-five per cent to Katherine Adams. At that time it was worth next to nothing, but once Maud had predeceased him it became quite a handy sum.'

'Wonder if the good doctor knew about this little benefit?' speculated Jackson artlessly. 'Now *that* would be a useful thing to find out.'

Harriet Lawson flounced out of Thorbeck's village store, her mouth pursed primly, then scurried along the street towards her terraced cottage facing the green. Two men were standing by the door; they seemed to be waiting for her.

She twisted her features into a preoccupied scowl as she approached them; if they were insurance men, they might get the message that she wasn't interested.

'Miss Lawson?' The voice of the taller one was quietly polite. He wore a dark grey suit, but there was no sign of the requisite briefcase, and his narrow mouth evinced only a token smile. The stout man beside him looked even less like an insurance salesman with his summer-weight tweed jacket. Her heart began to thud. 'We're police officers, Miss Lawson. May we come in?'

Montgomery had to duck his head under a malign pair of lintels in order to enter the tiny sitting-room. It was fusty and ill-lit, with a dead feel somehow emphasized by the solemn background ticking of a clock. A glossy magazine called *Looking after your Health* lent paradox, as did the distant glimpse of the sunlit greensward through the mullioned window.

'I've just been out for some things for my lunch,' said Harriet Lawson. 'These village shops really take advantage of folk like me who have no transport. Ask them for two ounces of ham and it's always: "Just over – is that all right?" *Never* under. It's the same with cheese. I call it exploitation.'

Her face was etched with the unattractive lines of long-standing disgruntlement and Montgomery felt he had her measure. She would be lucky to find a two-ounce pack in a supermarket, he thought. It would serve her right if the village storekeeper gave up the unequal struggle and abandoned the Harriets to their fate.

'There's no choice, either,' she grumbled. 'I wanted the small tin of butter beans, not the large. And the *price*...'

'At least the shop's convenient,' he said. 'Now, Miss Lawson, we've come to ask for your assistance with an inves-

147

tigation we are currently undertaking: it concerns the death of Mrs Maud Witherspoon, whom I think you knew.'

'Slightly.' Harriet gave a little toss of her head. 'She used to be connected with the Ladies' Friendship Guild, of which I am a member.'

'Ah, good. You'll know that she died suddenly ... We received letters at the station expressing reservations about the circumstances – and we have reason to believe that you were the author of those letters.'

He watched her closely; her mouth opened and her eyes blinked nervously, but there was no explosion of outraged innocence. After too long a pause, she seemed to realize that some comment was expected.

'What nonsense!' she said with another flick of the head. 'Why should I do a thing like that?'

'We're hoping you'll tell us.'

'I think you've got the wrong person, Inspector – Montgomery, is it? I know nothing about poor Maud's medical problems. She had a son who calls himself a doctor: why don't you ask *him* about it?'

Montgomery paused, preparatory to demolishing her stance, then heard a low call from his sergeant.

'Sir!'

William Bird had edged across to the window and now stood leaning over a pad of exercise papers on a nearby oak table. With three brisk strides Montgomery joined him.

'Look at this.'

The top sheet of the pad displayed a scattering of phrases and short sentences in the familiar niggardly handwriting. Words had been roughly deleted here and there, but the eye was drawn to a deeply gouged circle of biro at the bottom, and the two hate-filled lines it encompassed: *They're coming for you soon, you cow. It won't be Puerto de la Cruz for your NEXT long holiday.*

A stamped envelope was propped against an ugly porcelain jar in the centre of the table. Montgomery picked it up and perused it with slow deliberation; the addressee was a Mrs Gertrude Grant.

'More letters?' he asked Harriet, who stood greyly appalled across the room. 'My, you have been busy.'

It took only minutes to tap the well of Harriet's resentment for Gertrude; as they sat in dingy armchairs near the fireplace, two decades of venom poured out in an unstoppable flood:

'... She gave herself airs, but she was always common as muck. That "Weddell Grant" nonsense! She was plain Mrs Grant until that poor man died. He couldn't keep up with her demands, you see ... no, not *those* sort of demands, but clothes, and holidays, and posher cars than their neighbours. She had to be the first person in the LFG with a video, of course, and now it's satellite television ... What's that? Oh, her husband died of a heart attack. Brought on by *stress*, I'm convinced. He was her third husband; she'd buried two others when the luxuries started running low – did very nicely out of their wills, as well. You'd think she wouldn't need another penny, wouldn't you, but money runs through her fat fingers like water. She took herself off on a Caribbean cruise last year. Very nice, when some of us have never been abroad in our lives. This Easter it was three weeks in Tenerife ...'

'Miss Lawson,' chipped in Montgomery, 'I understand that Mrs Grant's lifestyle could be regarded as extravagant, and we've touched on her alleged misuse of charity funds – but do you really think she's capable of murder?'

'I certainly do. Three husbands, all dying like that? The second one was Eric Castle. He was a shy man who ran a music shop and did a lot for the Rotary Club. I used to meet him in the library on Mondays ... I *know* he was interested in me. Then Gertrude Grant had to come along and sink her hooks into him! He didn't last five years – and neither did the life insurance.'

Montgomery exchanged covert glances with Sergeant Bird.

'I was thinking more of Maud Witherspoon,' he said.

'Well, yes. It's just the same, isn't it? You've spoken to the Hope in the City staff – you know she needed money urgently. She persuaded Maud to change her will, then killed her.'

'Do you have any actual *proof*, Miss Lawson?'

149

She stared at him blankly. 'Proof?' she echoed. 'That's not up to me. That's your department!'

'She does have a point,' murmured Sergeant Bird as they drove away from Harriet's cramped cottage, leaving her smarting under the weight of a heavy rebuke from Montgomery.

'About proof? I know. Pull in round this corner, Will . . . I want us to pay another visit here in Thorbeck.'

Sergeant Bird parked the police Metro at the neck of the wide leafy cul-de-sac which led to Oaklands. 'I don't think the Witherspoons will be home at this time,' he said doubtfully. 'Lynn, perhaps.'

'We aren't going to see them. It's the neighbours I'm interested in.'

'They were canvassed as soon as Deborah disappeared.'

'I know – that's just it. Earnest young constables were knocking on doors asking when people had last seen Deborah, with or without cat. The enquiries weren't held in the context of George's murder. If a neighbour had seen someone else come to the house that Saturday afternoon, he may have been given no reason to volunteer the information.'

Montgomery stared down the road, his face growing tight. 'I thought of this yesterday when I was interviewing Katherine Adams, but it applies equally to Gertrude Grant. Miss Lawson has been a disappointment as far as hard evidence is concerned. We have to go back to basics, see what kind of alibi Gertrude offers us, and test it out. But it will strengthen our hand immensely if a neighbour has seen a large woman marching up the drive at the relevant time – or thrashing through the undergrowth at the back.'

'The houses and grounds are designed for privacy,' said Sergeant Bird.

'Yes, but when I was last at Oaklands I noticed that an extension built on the property to the left marginally over-looked them. Someone might just have been staring out of the window at the crucial time . . . we can but ask.'

Montgomery was to be disappointed; no one was at home in the large, cheerful-looking residence next to the Wither-spoons' house. He prowled around the garden for a few minutes, looking for gaps in the thick cypress border between the two properties, but came away shaking his head.

'We'll try again later,' he said.

'Where now?' asked William Bird when they had returned to the Metro.

'Dr Greaves's surgery, I think.' Dr Greaves was an elderly GP who did duty as police surgeon. Montgomery sucked in his lower lip in contemplation. 'Yes,' he decided. 'We'll go there. I want to find out more about these warfarin tablets, especially their colour. If Gertrude *is* responsible for Maud's death, then perhaps Jackson's idea isn't so unlikely after all; we haven't been able to come up with anything better. Perhaps there *were* pills of a similar colour in the room.'

'Venning Road is nearer,' said Sergeant Bird, raising an eyebrow.

'Dr Greaves, please.' Montgomery no longer felt he could trust any of Neville's partners. An outsider was the safest choice.

'Inspector Montgomery, isn't it?' Ian May, Dr Greaves's part-ner, greeted them with a friendly smile. 'We met when the old man let me tag along on that Bulwell case. I'm afraid he's visiting Scotland just now; can I help you?'

'Yes. Can you tell me the colour of warfarin tablets, please?'

'Warfarin ... What strength did you have in mind? One milligram? Three? Five?'

'Oh ... Whatever you'd call a normal dose.'

'There's no such thing; it depends on the individual. Some people need a lot – we call them "resistant" – while others need hardly any. All sorts of factors affect the way the body handles warfarin, you see ... things like whether you're a long-term alcoholic, or an epileptic on treatment...'

'Give me each of the colours and strengths, then.'

'Now you're asking. I remember the one-milligram tablets

are brown, and the three are blue, but the five? A pharmacist would know straight off. They dish out the things – we only prescribe them. Hang on a tick.' He opened a desk drawer and drew out a slim volume. At that moment his telephone rang.

'Here,' he said, thrusting the book at Montgomery. 'Have a butcher's yourself.'

He picked up the phone, and Montgomery gave his attention to the book, a softback entitled *British National Formulary*. It was a compendium of prescribable drugs, and gave details of their uses, side-effects and contra-indications. Warfarin duly appeared under the heading: 'Oral anticoagulants', and Montgomery began his reading from the top of this section.

The very first sentence was a shock: *Oral anticoagulants . . . take at least thirty-six to forty-eight hours for the anticoagulant effect to develop . . .*

'William!'

'Sergeant Bird followed Montgomery's pointing finger. 'Phew!' he whistled. 'Nothing I read about the drug said *that*. It totally changes the picture, doesn't it?'

Dr May finished his call and surveyed them beadily. 'You're both looking rather stunned,' he said. 'Anything I can do?'

'Is this an accepted fact?' asked Montgomery, showing him the paragraph.

'Oh, yes. Clotting's a complex process. There are lots of jolly little protein substances circulating in the bloodstream which work together to promote clot formation when an injury occurs; we'd bleed to death if they didn't. Sometimes, however, we want to prevent clots forming, or stop existing ones getting bigger. Then we use drugs which block the actions of these proteins. Warfarin is best for long-term use, but takes time to achieve its full effect. If we want rapid action, the drug heparin is usually chosen, although it only works by injection.'

He beamed as Montgomery made rapid mental adjustments to his conceptions of the Witherspoon case. Gertrude wouldn't have needed to practise hazardous sleight of hand in order to ensure that Maud didn't die until the Friday; it was all there in the pills.

'Thank you,' he said, starting for the door. 'You've been very helpful.'

'I can get hold of some samples if you like,' Dr May called after them as they left. 'Just give me a call.'

Montgomery lifted a hand in acknowledgement, but he was scarcely listening; the specific colour of the warfarin was no longer important.

On their return to Thorbeck they found that the house next to Oaklands was now teeming with activity. The owner, an architect, introduced himself as Damien Balfour; his three children, a boy and two girls, stared with unabashed interest at the detectives, while his pretty wife was better able to conceal her curiosity.

'We were working in the garden that Saturday,' he said, 'well, *some* of us were!' His youngest daughter lowered her head and giggled from behind a curtain of long flaxen hair.

'Did you see any visitors entering or leaving Dr Wither-spoon's house between, say, two and four o'clock?' asked Montgomery.

'I'm afraid we weren't really watching. We had enough excitement on our own side of the fence.'

The little girl chortled again. 'Henry got stuck!' she announced.

'What's that?' Montgomery took a step towards her, then inwardly cursed himself as alarm flared in her eyes. His eager-ness must have shown too clearly. Forcing himself to take time, he smiled at her. 'Is that Henry the cat?' he asked pleasantly.

She sucked her thumb and turned away.

'He's not our cat,' explained Mr Balfour. 'He belongs to Dr Witherspoon's daughter, but he often sneaks into our garden when our own cat is inside; the usual territorial one-upman-ship. That Saturday he caused quite a stir; he was stranded in our sycamore all afternoon!'

153

17

Montgomery wondered if he could possibly look as foolish as he felt. This shock, coming so soon after the previous one, had paralysed his senses. The entire circumstantial basis for George's death had just crashed around his ears; he felt incapable of rational thought. *Another cat . . . ?*

The sight of William Bird, usually so imperturbable, now resembling a moonstruck imbecile, jolted him back to full function.

'Flycatching, Will?' he enquired.

Sergeant Bird snapped his jaw shut, and blinked. 'This is – very odd, sir,' he faltered.

'Indeed.' Montgomery faced Damien Balfour once more. 'Would you be kind enough to show us the tree, and describe the incident?' he asked.

'Of course.'

They all trooped out to the garden and halted below a majestic sycamore growing ten yards from the border with Dr Witherspoon's grounds. It was a sturdy tree with many side-branches, ideal for young children to climb. Evidence of its popularity was discernible in the shape of a partially built tree house, a hideaway high in the leafy cool above.

'We saw Henry sniffing round the base of the tree about half past one,' said Mr Balfour. 'Then a few minutes later, he climbed up to the platform. Young Gavin here decided to play with him – didn't you, lad? – but unfortunately Henry took fright and went right out along that narrow branch. It was dipping and swaying, and the cat was hanging on with his claws . . .'

154

'Sorry to interrupt,' said Montgomery, 'but can you be exact about the time here?'

'Well . . . somewhere around two o'clock.'

'Mrs Witherspoon could tell you,' piped up Gavin. 'She was just going out.'

'You saw her?'

'Yes. Dr Witherspoon was waiting in his car, and she got in, then she went back for her hat, then eventually they drove away.'

Montgomery held his breath. 'Are you *sure* about this, Gavin? How long was she inside?'

'About ten minutes. That's right, isn't it, Dad?'

Montgomery swung his intent gaze to Mr Balfour. Lynn Witherspoon . . . so *right* as a suspect, and yet so wrong . . .

Damien Balfour nodded. 'I'd say so. I was up the tree myself by then, trying to encourage Henry back towards *terra firma*. Gavin nudged me and asked if Mrs Witherspoon was going to a wedding, because she was all dressed up. I peered across and saw that she was wearing a full-skirted dress in an unusual shade of cream; it was most attractive.' He coloured. 'You'll have to forgive our nosiness, Inspector. The truth is Lynn Witherspoon usually looks rather dowdy, so we were curious about the change . . . Anyway, she returned to the house and emerged ten minutes later, as Gavin says, with a wide-brimmed sun-hat. The day *was* a scorcher.

'Our efforts to help Henry seemed to be counterproductive, so we climbed down the tree again and got on with our gardening. But my wife wasn't happy; by four o'clock she was insisting we call the RSPCA!'

Mrs Balfour gave a small, embarrassed smile. 'Henry looked so unhappy,' she said. 'With most cats you know they'll find their own way down, but Henry is plump and clumsy, and he tends to get into difficulties. We were amazed he'd managed to climb so far up the tree in the first place; as the afternoon wore on we became convinced he was stuck. We didn't have a ladder long enough to reach him.'

'*I* said we should send for the fire brigade,' chirruped Gavin.

'And *I* said we should stretch out the hammock underneath,' said the eldest of his two small sisters.

'What happened?' asked Montgomery.

'Oh, we gave him a bit longer,' answered Mr Balfour. 'About half past four he started backing along the branch in an ungainly fashion, ears flattened, scrabbling periodically when he lost his grip. When he reached the trunk, he half-slid, half-ran down it to the tree house; it was easy from there.'

'You're certain this was as late as half past four?' asked Sergeant Bird.

'Absolutely. It may have been a quarter to five.'

'Did you see *anyone at all* enter Dr Witherspoon's house at *any time* during the afternoon, once he had left with Mrs Witherspoon?'

'No; we were down here in the garden. You can't see past that thick cypress hedge.'

That was true. With Gavin's loftily granted permission, Montgomery made his own brief check of the field of vision afforded by the tree house, then the two detectives took their leave. They were both sadly puzzled.

'Do you want to go home, Will?'

They had been sitting in the car for fifteen minutes, each silently trying to make sense of the day's events.

Sergeant Bird gave Montgomery a knowing look. 'From that I deduce that you're going to carry on tonight.'

'Yes . . . I must. The more complex this becomes the more I feel it's vital that we find Deborah. Maybe she's just a mixed-up adolescent, or maybe she's something worse, but stopping her from harming herself is more important than trying to right past wrongs when the way is so obscure.'

'Count me in,' said Sergeant Bird. 'If we can just stop for a cuppa and a slice of toast, I'm all yours.'

'Can you wait half an hour? I want to go to Sneinton Terrace while we're still on this side of town.'

'Ray Cooper's place?' William Bird gave a gusty sigh of resignation. 'I suppose I can keep the pangs at bay for a while.'

*

Montgomery was thoughtful as they drove along the shabby street to the address where Martin Witherspoon would hopefully be found. He had tried to imagine himself in Deborah's situation, and concluded that a visit to Oaklands would simply have wasted time. No; if Deborah was confiding in anyone, it would be Aileen or her brother. He had reservations about young Aileen; she was undoubtedly a loyal friend to Deborah, but there lay the problem: loyalty could prove obstructive, be used as a justification for twisting the truth. Re-educating Aileen might take too long. That left Martin, and although Montgomery had no reason to think that Martin and Deborah were close, her options seemed to him severely limited.

The door of number three had no bell; Sergeant Bird knocked briskly and stood back to wait. From a window above came aggressive, discordant sounds, minority modern music which made Montgomery cringe and wonder how loud it was inside. He was glad that William was with him. The big sergeant gave unstintingly of his time after hours, needing only an occasional top-up of food to keep going; someone like Jackson would have been whingeing about overtime pay by now.

In response to a second, even more authoritative tattoo, the door opened and a girl glared out at them. She had lank, close-cropped dark hair, and the long baggy jumper above her frayed jeans was none too clean. Four brass studs formed a crescent above her left earlobe.

'What d'yer want?' she asked truculently.

'We'd like to see Martin, please, if he's in.'

Her eyes narrowed as she squinted at each of them in turn. ''Oo wants 'im?'

'I'm Detective Inspector Montgomery; this is Detective Sergeant Bird. Martin has met us before.'

'Sorry.' She gave a cold leer. ''E's not in right now.'

She made as if to close the door, but hesitated as Montgomery used his most commanding tone: 'We'll speak to Ray, then, if you don't mind.'

With an ill grace she suggested they wait, and a minute later Ray Cooper appeared.

'You still after Martin?' he asked. 'He's done nowt wrong as far as I know. Why don't you give it a rest?'

'We need his help,' said Montgomery. 'We're trying to trace his sister Deborah, and we're hoping she may have contacted him. That's the sole reason we're here.'

Something flickered at the back of Ray's eyes, and was gone; he frowned doubtfully. 'I suppose you'd better come in,' he said. The house smelt of bolognese sauce, and the threadbare carpet in the sitting-room was largely hidden under an ankle-deep swill of newspapers, discarded beer cans, cushions and clothes. Montgomery reiterated his objective for the benefit of the girl, and learned that her name was Josie. Ray was the nominal tenant in the house; he lived downstairs while the upstairs bedrooms were sublet, probably illegally, to a student couple and to Martin. If it wasn't for the telephone, Montgomery would have suspected that he was standing in a squat.

''S a pity you didn't come an hour ago,' observed the girl. 'Deborah *did* ring; it's the first time 'e's 'eard from 'er.'

'What did she say?' Montgomery's reasoning had proved correct; this was very promising.

'Dunno. We weren't listening in. We were 'avin' our meal in the kitchen.'

'Did Martin say where she was ringing from?'

'We didn't talk about it.'

'Has he gone to meet her?'

'Look, Mr Montgomery, we don't *know*.' This was from Ray. 'Martin used to be a real mate of mine. He'd come down the pub and have a few beers, or we'd go for a bop at the club on Saturday nights. But recently he's kept much more to himself. I don't know what he does. Or where he goes. He's his own man.'

Was Martin outgrowing his grand rebellion? wondered Montgomery. If he possessed intelligence, as Mrs Blanchard had reported, then there was little to stimulate him in the present company, while the students would merely remind him of opportunities he'd squandered. His behaviour was understandable. This residence was a temporary expedient, and it wouldn't be too surprising to hear in the near future that he had changed his job and moved on.

At Montgomery's side William Bird spoke up, his measured tones competing with the fierce, eerie music from above.

'We're very worried about Deborah,' he said.

He was looking straight at Josie; she dropped her own gaze, then cleared her throat.

''E might be wi' Bev,' she volunteered.

'Who is Bev?'

'Beverley. Beverley Taylor, 'is girl friend.'

'She isn't,' contradicted Ray. 'Hasn't been for months.'

'Yes, she 'as!'

'Where might we find Beverley?' broke in Montgomery.

'She lives wi' 'er mum in Aspley Towers: flat ninety-two. But she might not be there . . . There's a house she used to go to wi' Martin – Colliery Street. Three doors down from the pub. It's condemned, but I think they still use it.'

Thanking Josie, the detectives left, and decided on the closer destination of Aspley Towers. It was an unremarkable block of council flats, built during the sixties to provide a short-term solution to a long-term problem. They took the lift into its cheerless interior, and knocked on Mrs Taylor's door.

There was a long delay before the door opened and a woman with straggling bleached hair asked them their business. She clutched a dressing-gown tightly round her thin frame, and the polished toe-nails peeping out from the mules on her feet seemed to mock her sallow-grey skin.

Montgomery introduced himself quietly, so her neighbours wouldn't hear. 'We're looking for a friend of Beverley's,' he said, 'and we're hoping Beverley might help us. Is she at home?'

The woman gave a sarcastic laugh. 'Yer must be jokin'! I 'aven't seen the little tramp for two days. I can't tell yer where she is – I'm only 'er mother!'

'Did you report her missing?'

She shrugged. 'Why waste yer time? She's run off before. Last time it were three days. Well, I've told 'er – if she comes back pregnant, she's out on 'er ear. I'm not lookin' after any brats.'

A man appeared in the passage behind her, a bulky, unkempt individual with a burgeoning beer belly. He squinted at them with Neanderthal menace, at the same time tugging at the zip on his trousers.

'Are these men botherin' yer, Rose? Want me ter get rid of 'em?'

'We're police,' snapped Montgomery.

With wondrous alacrity, the man melted into the background shadows, and Montgomery appealed again to Mrs Taylor. 'Can you tell us any of Beverley's haunts – any pubs she might go to, or friends she might be with?'

'No, sorry.' She looked totally uninterested. 'Now, if that's all . . .'

As the lift clanked noisily up to their floor, Montgomery felt a profound sense of desolation. For all his faults, Neville Witherspoon was a loving, caring father. Deborah may have found his rules irksome, but her situation had surely been infinitely better than Beverley's. How did the old saying go? 'When you have sons, you worry; when you have daughters, you pray.' Montgomery himself had one of each, and in that dismal corridor of Aspley Towers the thought came to him bleak as winter, and certain as death: no one was praying for Beverley.

'Colliery Street,' read Sergeant Bird, peering up at the dingy sign on the side-wall of the Jubilee. The fading light lent a forbidding air to the dilapidated houses; across the street they were at least inhabited, as evidenced by curtains and window-sill ornaments, but the terrace stretching away from the pub had boarded-up windows and peeling doors defaced by slogans.

'Makes Sneinton Terrace look pretty desirable,' he muttered.

Montgomery walked slowly to the third door and assessed that particular house. It was the most intact in the row, but was scarcely more salubrious than its neighbours. Thick planks had been nailed across both window and door at the

160

front; a debris of cardboard and broken roof tiles spattered the pavement outside.

The street was uncannily silent. It was hard to imagine that anyone had ever lived in these shells: laughed, eaten dinner, watched television . . . and in their present form they were a vile place for a tryst.

'Let's try the back,' said Montgomery. He led the way along a narrow passage between the houses and unlatched a squeaking wooden gate to enter a small, stone-flagged yard. A brick wash-house and outside toilet projected from the kitchen, their windows grimy and cracked.

Montgomery turned the handle on the back door and gave a push with his shoulder. The door opened stiffly and crunched against a broken milk bottle just inside.

'Hello!' called Montgomery. 'Is anyone here?' Only a thin echo of his own voice bounced back at him.

Sergeant Bird was breathing against his neck. 'They might be too frightened to answer, sir.'

'More likely they're in some warm pub. Well, let's do the job properly regardless.'

He stepped over the threshold, avoiding the glass, and walked across the chipped linoleum into the hall. Remnants of garish paper hung from the walls, but there was no sign of human habitation either here or in the blacked-out front room.

The uncarpeted stairs amplified every footfall as the two men ascended to the landing, where shadows lay across the bare floorboards. They stopped; nothing stirred.

'Hello!' called Montgomery again.

William Bird shook his head and began to retrace his steps, but Montgomery was thorough by nature. He checked the front bedroom – empty – then turned his attention to the small room at the back . . .

'My God.'

Sergeant Bird heard Montgomery's sickened protest, and hurried to join him, his feet clumping against the hard floor.

Wan light from the dirty sash window grudgingly illuminated the body of a girl. She lay jack-knifed in an agonized foetal position, her face hidden, and the bunched-up quilt under her pathetically skinny hips was dark with blood.

The sergeant paused, stricken; for all his professional training he could go no further. Echoes of his upbringing conspired with a deeper atavism to mould his unconscious response to the tragic sight: they took his unresisting hands, and branded the palms together.

18

Montgomery, too, was fighting against strong feelings, and knelt down by the body with heavy reluctance. He saw without surprise the long, vicious knitting-needle, bloodied at the tip, which lurked in a fold of the quilt. He noted a vacuum flask, a storm-lantern and a plastic box of food. There was something else he thought he might find . . .

'Is it Deborah, sir?'

William Bird's voice sounded calm as usual, but Montgomery knew his friend found this death as affecting as he did.

'No. This must be Beverley Taylor. She's much shorter, and the face bears no resemblance to Deborah's photograph.' The girl wore a cheap watch and turquoise ring; carefully he removed them from the limp hand and slid them into a plastic bag for identification purposes. Meanwhile, William Bird crouched down beside him.

'Did she do this herself?' he mused.

'I imagine so.'

'There's such a lot of blood: the quilt is soaked through. Strange that it hasn't clotted . . . When do you think she died?'

Montgomery gently flexed the unresisting limbs. 'Rigor hasn't started yet. She's cold, though . . . I'd say mid to late afternoon.'

'What a way to go in this day and age!'

And what a place, thought Montgomery. He busied himself searching the room, a rapid but painstaking sweep which included the lunchbox and Beverley's scratched plastic handbag. In the depths of a side-pocket his diligence was rewarded;

163

he withdrew a folded buff envelope, opened the flap and tapped the edge against his hand: out rolled a single, scored blue tablet.

'Warfarin, three milligrams,' he said.

William Bird's eyes widened in comprehension. 'I've been slow,' he began. 'I couldn't believe that Deborah was really capable of such things . . .'

'No, Will.' For once Montgomery was ahead of his sergeant, and the realization gave him no pleasure. 'Not Deborah. It's Martin; it's been Martin all along.'

Josie's chalk-white face was streaked with tears.

'Yeah, these are Bev's things,' she said. 'Why did she 'ave to die? 'E said it would be orright.'

They sat at the kitchen table in Sneinton Terrace, surrounded by glutinous pots and pans, while Ray hovered uneasily in the background.

'Would you excuse us for a few minutes?' Montgomery asked him. 'Perhaps you could ask your lodgers upstairs to turn down their music?' Josie knew more than she had so far admitted, he was sure, and without Ray's inhibiting presence might be encouraged to talk. 'Now, Josie,' he said as blessed peace descended, 'tell us about Bev and Martin.'

She blew her nose. 'They've been goin' together for years. 'E used to take 'er down the Palais, an' to the flicks – yer know, all the usual stuff. But then 'e started on them fruit machines and didn't 'ave no time for 'er. 'E made 'er really un'appy. She used to come an' talk to me about it.' She glanced up at the two detectives and saw that they were listening attentively.

'Bev said 'e'd changed, but I weren't so sure: I never felt that comfortable wi' Martin. Anyway, she wanted to get 'im back, even when 'e'd begun spendin' all 'is Sat'dy nights in't casino. She'd lend 'im money, she were that besotted. And yer don't earn much workin' be'ind counter at *Kiddietogs*!

'They did get together again, at Easter, then Bev found that she were expectin' a baby an' 'e didn't want to know. 'E said it weren't 'is, but it were. If you ask me, I think she did it

164

deliberate, so 'e'd stay with 'er, but it didn't work. 'E were meetin' really glamorous women at the casino by then, older women, so 'e didn't want Bev 'angin' around.'

'Did he know anything about her plans for the pregnancy?' asked Montgomery.

''Course 'e did; it were 'is idea. She got scared, yer see, and asked 'im to 'elp 'er. 'E said she couldn't go to the 'ospital, because 'is dad knew the surgeons there and 'e might get to 'ear about the baby. 'E said 'e'd get 'er some pills which would do the trick, if she'd do somethin' for 'im.'

Montgomery had a shrewd idea about the nature of this *quid pro quo*. Examples of Martin's unholy cunning had been filtering from his subconscious ever since the evening's grim discovery.

''E wanted 'er to make some sorter telephone call,' went on Josie. 'I don't know exactly what, but she said it were wicked and she wouldn't do it. She were right upset. I can't tell yer no more; I didn't see 'er after that.'

'Thank you for being so frank, Josie,' said Montgomery, rising from the table. 'Now it's very important that we find Martin. Have you the *slightest* idea where he might have gone tonight?'

She shook her head.

'May we see his room?'

'Yer'd best ask Ray. I'm only visitin'.'

Ray's half-hearted assent was good enough for Montgomery. He wasn't hopeful of the outcome, but any clue as to Martin's current whereabouts was worth following up. Time was not on their side; the obvious sequel to that telephone call was as monstrous as it was logical.

'There's nothing here,' said Sergeant Bird. 'No diary, address book or scribbled note.' He held out a multisided gaming chip. 'It's true about the casino.'

'I didn't doubt it. It explains so much – hang on. What's that in the corner?'

A screwed-up piece of paper lay between a battered chest of drawers and the wall. Montgomery darted across the room, picked it up and unfolded the ball, smoothing it out carefully against the surface of a nearby table.

'This is Deborah's writing!' he said tersely.

'And the paper looks like part of a school exercise book,' added Sergeant Bird. The same recollection flashed through both their minds: a physics notebook with its central pages missing . . .

'Can you read it, sir?'

'Just about.' He frowned. *'Dear Mother and Father, I'm so sorry about Uncle George. You've got to forgive Henry. He didn't mean any harm – it must have been an accident. I can't let you kill him, so I'm taking him away. Please don't try to find us. I'll ring when the time . . .* That's funny – the message is incomplete. The bottom part of the page has been torn away. I don't like this, Will. I don't like it at all.'

'You think Martin has the other half?'

'He took this note from her bedroom on the day George died, yet he didn't destroy it. We must conclude that he intends to use it to further his purpose. If he's gone to meet Deborah somewhere tonight, then she's in real danger!'

'His own sister?'

'That's just the point – she's not his sister. There's no blood tie between them whatsoever. She's the perfect scapegoat . . . Come on!' He swung decisively out of the door and hurried past the students' bedroom, from where the sweetish smoke of lesser sins than murder oozed through the cracks around the door.

'Where are we going?'

'Aileen Blanchard's home – she's our only hope.'

Montgomery took the wheel and drove swiftly through the darkening streets, his brain alive to the battering of self-recrimination.

'Is he good?' Martin had asked. It hadn't been an idle question. He had wanted to be quite certain that the police would check his alibi thoroughly, designate any involvement in the death of George a physical impossibility, and note how many facets of his 'confession' were more applicable to Deborah.

Out of necessity he had laid a trail – and they had dutifully followed, every inch of the way . . .

'No, he isn't good,' murmured Montgomery under his breath. 'He's ordinary, which isn't good enough.' Only finding Deborah alive would bring expiation; he hoped the hollow ache beneath his diaphragm was not a harbinger of impending disaster.

'I don't know anything!' said Aileen defiantly.

The Blanchards had been watching television *en famille* when the two detectives arrived on their doorstep. Now, after some initial difficulty, Montgomery had managed to employ his Sneinton Terrace tactics, and interview Aileen in the kitchen with only her mother present.

'We think that Deborah is in great danger,' he said to her. 'You're her friend; you're the one she'd turn to. Won't you give us any help at all towards finding her?'

Aileen tilted her nose into the air, but her eyes were uncertain. 'Why should she be in danger? She's only trying to protect Henry – I should imagine,' she added hastily.

'Lovey, you must tell us if you know where she is,' urged Mrs Blanchard.

'I don't – but I'm sure when she feels it's safe for Henry she'll come back.'

'Aileen . . . ' Montgomery leaned forward. 'A girl is dead. We found her tonight. We think the person who caused her death is after Deborah right now. We can't waste a moment if we're to help her.'

Aileen looked stricken, but gamely stuck to her pseudo-hypothetical line.

'Deborah wouldn't go out to meet a stranger at night,' she said. 'Only someone she knew well.'

Montgomery had to be brutal. 'The dead girl is Martin's girl friend Beverley. We strongly suspect he means to harm Deborah, and we know she rang him tonight. Your loyalty does you great credit, Aileen, but right now it's misplaced, badly so. It's vital that we all work together to avoid a tragedy.'

Aileen drew back from him and looked wildly at the three faces ranged against her. 'How do I know whether to believe you?' she cried. 'I – I don't know what to say.'

Sergeant Bird quietly drew alongside Mrs Blanchard. 'May we take a look in your garden shed, please?' he asked.

She was startled. 'Of – of course. Would you like a torch?'

'I've got one, thank you.'

Aileen opened her mouth to protest, but found no words. Dazedly she trailed after them as they picked their way along the path in the failing light, reached the new wooden shed and threw open the door. The interior was in deep shadow.

'There's an electric light switch to the right,' said Mrs Blanchard. 'Let me ... ' She pressed the switch, and the entire contents of the shed sprang into bright relief. They saw boxes, cushions, books, bottled water, a sleeping bag, a bucket ... only the occupant of the cosy den was missing.

Mrs Blanchard swung round. 'Aileen!' she shouted. 'How could you lie all this time?'

'I didn't, I didn't!' Tears poured down Aileen's cheeks. 'When you asked me before, I said "Cross my heart and hope to die" and I *never* break that! I didn't know where she'd gone. She said she was going to find a bed and breakfast place.'

'You looked after Henry, though, on Saturday night,' said Sergeant Bird. 'He was here, and Austin knew.'

'"The dog in the night-time",' murmured Montgomery.

'Yes – except that this one barked.'

Aileen sullenly nodded her head. 'I did try to help her. They were going to *kill* Henry. Deborah was frantic. Her dad's not normal – he'd really do something like that.'

They returned to the kitchen, where Montgomery saw that Mrs Blanchard's fury was threatening to re-erupt in purplish splendour. Quickly he stepped in. 'Aileen,' he said, his tone earnest but kindly, 'believe me when I say that Deborah is in real danger. It's not just a ploy we're using to get you to betray her – we don't work like that. We understand Deborah's worries about Henry, and I'm confident we can sort them out, but right now Deborah's own safety is much more important. We think she's gone to meet Martin – has she?'

'Yes,' whispered Aileen. 'She went to the phone box round

168

the corner tonight and rang Ray Cooper's house to ask if he would speak to Martin at work. But Martin was there himself. He gave Deborah directions to a place where they could talk without anyone seeing or hearing them. It's near a railway line, that's all she told me. I said she could take my bike, and she has done. But I don't know where she's gone, truly . . . I wish I did.'

Montgomery slammed shut the door of the Metro and reached for a map of Nottingham.

'We have a nice line in reducing young girls to tears, don't we?' he said bleakly.

'I think it's more a case of *exitus acta probat*.' William Bird was ever lenitive.

'What's that? Breaking eggs to make omelettes?'

'Almost. "The result validates the deed" – in other words, the end justifies the means.'

'Hah! Would that it did. Have we the remotest idea where Martin is – apart from near a railway track with lethal intent?'

He tugged the map open with a loud rustle, but lowered it to his knees after a cursory glance. A map could only give him a number of options; they needed precision. For that he must put himself in Martin's shoes, limit himself to Martin's own experience, and avoid any over-anxious clouding of the issue. It had worked for Deborah, it would work again.

Empathize . . .

Suddenly everything was clear. He was Martin, digging a trench in an old man's allotment, the sun beating on his back. He was Martin, thinking quickly, enmeshed in a murder enquiry he had never anticipated – and he was Martin, grimly determined to aim for the ultimate prize, the entire inheritance, and simultaneously incriminate his naïve adoptive sister.

He was going to kill Deborah and make it look like suicide. He needed a stretch of railway line where he could give a sudden push from a concealed vantage point, a bridge or a hillside, a place where the driver of any oncoming train would have no time to react. And he had been staring at just such a place every Saturday afternoon for weeks . . .

Montgomery snapped his seat-belt into position and started the engine.

'Where are we going?' asked Sergeant Bird.

'Mr Lampkin's locality,' he answered. 'I think we can repay him for the beans.'

19

Dusk was well advanced by the time Montgomery rolled the Metro to a discreet halt in a side-street across the road from Mr Lampkin's bungalow. In twenty minutes, he estimated, it would be too dark to see anything useful; they would have no second chance.

'Can you remember the layout below Mr Lampkin's allotment?' he asked Sergeant Bird. 'Any paths or open spaces leading down to the line?'

'There *is* a track,' answered the sergeant thoughtfully. 'It runs parallel to the line a few feet up the slope . . . but I don't recall any access to it from this area.'

'People must be able to get to their allotments.' Montgomery climbed out of the car, locked it, walked to the corner and pointed past the neat row of bungalows opposite. 'We should find an alleyway somewhere along there,' he said. 'The tunnel's in that direction, too.'

They crossed the road and kept silence past the Lampkins' home; the curtains in the bungalow were already drawn, and twilight had drained the welcome of the 'Glenfiddich' bushes. Sure enough, after fifty yards they came upon a NO CYCLING sign; a cinder track started here, wound between two of the dwellings and vanished behind a garden shed.

'This way,' hissed Montgomery. He broke into a trot but stopped within seconds as a giggle reached his ear, and detained William Bird with a brisk gesture. Treading as carefully as possible on the irritating cinders, he drew level with the corner of the shed; a young couple were leaning against the timber wall, writhing and murmuring, totally engrossed in each other's company. By no stretch of the imagination could they be Martin and Deborah.

Signalling Sergeant Bird to follow, Montgomery resumed his jog as the path swung right and took a gentle downturn. He didn't stop until they had reached the last allotment hut, where a gleam of silver caught his attention.

'What's that – a bike?' whispered Sergeant Bird.

'Yes. It's quite small: a ladies' bike; I wonder if it's Aileen's?' Montgomery peered along the embankment, but there was no sign of the bicycle's owner. All he could see was the fence bordering the last allotment and its immediate environs: on the one side, fuscous earth with its leafy sproutings, on the other, grass, a spread more indigo than green as it bumped and rippled its way down to the track. Already it was too dark to make out the tunnel mouth beyond; if anyone stood in its vicinity, only short-range inspection would identify them.

He scrambled down the increasingly treacherous path, Sergeant Bird puffing behind, and halted at its intersection with another.

'This is the path I remembered, sir,' gasped Sergeant Bird. 'It goes part way towards the tunnel mouth, then peters out as the embankment steepens.'

'We'll take it,' said Montgomery. 'Keep quiet, and don't use your torch whatever the temptation. We mustn't announce our arrival.'

To whom? he wondered wryly. Another courting couple? That bicycle had given him fleeting hope, yet he knew if he dared face the situation squarely that the odds were stacked against a successful outcome. Martin had already displayed amazing ruthlessness and cunning. He could even now be on some railway platform, Beeston perhaps, joining in the communal horror at a young girl's sad accident. (But Aileen had said a *line*, not a station ...) He might be wallowing in the sweet smoke of Sneinton Terrace, calculating how long it would take Mr Barton to convert Maud Witherspoon's substantial estate into capital for squandering at the casino. Rivulets of money ... a haemorrhage of dissipation.

Montgomery found that he had begun to run again. Daylight was dying around him, and his fear of alerting Martin was subordinate to the deeper fear of reaching him too late. When was the next train due? How much warning would there be if it came from the tunnel? This had to be the right place; there was no margin for error.

He slowed up, and felt the spiteful sting as his hand brushed past a nettle. For a moment he had imagined there were voices ahead ... was he talking to himself? No, there they were again. Close; very close. A girl's voice, high-pitched, arguing – and the deeper tones of a man. He strained his ears to try to discern whether this was Martin; wishful thinking certainly decreed that it was. Where *were* they?

The harder he peered up the path, the less he was able to see. Montgomery twisted his head round to warn William Bird and, in the moment of turning, caught an image of two figures, a split-second flash on the retina, straight ahead. Of course: at night peripheral vision held superiority.

Sergeant Bird joined him and nodded to indicate that he could hear the voices; slowly they crept forward until the two figures were clearly visible in the gloaming.

'Not until you can promise that Henry will be safe. Please try again; they've got to listen. I'm going back now, Martin. I don't like it here ...'

The girl swung round and began to walk decisively towards the detectives. Sergeant Bird shrank behind the nearest wall of nettles, but Montgomery crawled up the bank so he could watch Martin. To his horror, he found that the boy had picked up an object from the side of the line, something large and heavy-looking, and was striding after Deborah, his hand aloft. Montgomery sprang to his feet.

'Martin!' he shouted. 'Martin Witherspoon. Put that down!'

The boy stopped as if galvanized, then stared about him fiercely to locate the source of the command. Something fell to the ground with a metallic clang. He walked away from the spot and began to laugh.

'All right, Inspector, you've caught us. But I'm afraid Deborah isn't quite ready to give herself up. I've been trying to persuade her.'

'Be quiet and stay there. Will, may I have your torch, please?'

Sergeant Bird appeared leading Deborah, who looked frightened and bemused. He tossed the torch to Montgomery.

'What were you carrying just now?' Montgomery asked Martin.

'Nothing.'

'Come off it. "Nothing" doesn't make a noise like an anvil.'

'OK . . . it was just a piece of junk I was curious about.'

'Indeed.' Briskly he quartered the ground with the torch-beam and soon came upon a rusty iron bar. 'Was it this?' he asked, lifting and illuminating it so that Martin could see.

'Might have been. I'm not sure. I was only fiddling about.'

Montgomery dropped the bar and came close to Martin. 'I'd like you to show me the contents of your pockets, please,' he said.

'You've got no right to ask that.'

'I'm afraid I have, as Sergeant Bird here will confirm.'

'Police and Criminal Evidence Act 1984,' murmured William Bird. 'Powers to stop and search – '

'Excuse me.' The voice, an uncertain treble, was Deborah's. Her eyes were wide and they could see the tremor in her hands. 'Please,' she faltered, 'this is all my fault. M-Martin's only trying to help me. Don't be angry with him.'

'You don't have to tell them anything, Debs.' Martin smiled at her and held out his arm; her face expressed astonishment, then she ran to him and buried it in his shoulder. Above the dishevelled hair, his lips curled in ironic triumph.

Montgomery was thinking fast; was there already enough evidence for an arrest, or was it all too circumstantial? He could hardly have waited for the attempt on Deborah's life to come to fruition in order to catch Martin red-handed, and what did the rest amount to? Josie's story was damning, but it was also hearsay. There might or might not be fingerprints on the warfarin envelope from Colliery Street, and a hunch of his about Mr Lampkin might prove misguided . . .

'I'll just remind you,' he said to Martin, 'I'm Detective Inspector Montgomery of the Nottinghamshire Police. You've been in the station and you've seen my identity, but here it is if you want a further look. I should like to see the contents of

174

your pockets because I believe you may be concealing an offensive weapon.'

Deborah gasped, but Martin grinned, visibly relaxing.

'If it makes you happy,' he said, 'here you are.' He peeled off his leather jacket and handed it to Montgomery, then turned out his trouser pockets and dumped the coins and handkerchiefs thus unearthed in Sergeant Bird's large hands.

Montgomery felt sweat dribble between his shoulder blades despite the growing cool of the night. The flatness of each jacket pocket confirmed his real belief that the presence of a weapon was unlikely; the true prize was something quite different. If it couldn't be found, the ensuing stalemate would be very hard to handle.

In the last pocket his fingers felt a folded strip of paper. He drew it out with great care, holding only the corner, and saw with a mental sigh of relief that it was ruled. Partially turning away from Martin, he shone the torch down, opened the packet and read the few scribbled words: *Please forgive me, Mother and Father. This is all I can think of to do. Your loving daughter, Deborah.*

'Well?' came a voice from behind him. 'Any knuckle-dusters?'

Montgomery faced them again and quietly addressed Deborah.

'Would you come here for a moment, Deborah?' he asked.

She clung on to Martin and shook her head.

'All right . . . ' Montgomery held out the paper for her to see. 'Is this your writing?'

'Y-yes. But I don't understand . . . ' She stared wildly up at Martin, whose cocksure leer had evaporated in an instant. 'Martin . . . ?'

'They planted it, you silly bitch.' He stepped backwards, appeared to stumble, and crouched to steady himself. The next moment, he had pulled something from his sock: there was a click, and a slender blade leapt gleaming into the torchlight.

Montgomery started forward, but he was too late; Martin had seized Deborah again, roughly this time, and was now holding the knife at her throat. She gave a little shriek.

175

'Let her go,' said Montgomery calmly. 'This won't help.'

'Like hell. You think you're so clever, don't you? So f——
clever.'

'We can talk about it if you put the knife down. I know you
felt you had a raw deal at home, but it wasn't Deborah's fault.'

'No?' Montgomery had lowered the torch-beam to the path;
in the dark they couldn't see Martin's eyes, but they could feel
the hatred glaring from them, hatred which vibrated in his
voice. 'Little Miss Perfect,' he mocked. '"Yes, Father, I'd *love* a
chemistry set. I'm going to be a doctor, just like you." And she
called *me* a hypocrite! But dear Deborah always aims to please.
She minces off to church on Sundays so that all Thorbeck can
see what an *exemplary* family their GP has. Image is all, isn't it,
Debs?'

Deborah stood mute, rigid with fear.

'She's always neat, clean and on time. Well done! Martin?
Oh, no one gives a toss what he does. In fact, he'd do
everyone a favour by taking himself as far away as possible.'

A faint croak escaped from Deborah. She coughed. 'That's –
not – true. Mother and Father worry about you.'

'Worry? Yes – I believe that. They worry about their
precious reputations. Why didn't you use the word "care",
Debs dear? Perhaps you're not such a hypocrite after all. Or is
it just that you don't have a sense of humour? Care's a funny
word – laugh!' He thrust the edge of the knife deeper against
the side of her neck, and she mewed in terror. 'Maybe it isn't
so funny after all. Let's try "love". That's a real rib-tickler. Go
on – give me a belly-laugh. Tell me that Mother and Father
love me!'

Deborah wept.

'Martin – ' began Montgomery.

'You shut up! Listen to her, crying with laughter. It's funny,
isn't it? It's hilarious. Of course Mother doesn't love me: she
isn't my f—— mother!'

There was silence, broken only by tearing sobs from
Deborah.

'Martin, let's talk about this somewhere more comfortable.
The car if you like; we're parked up on the road ... ' Montgomery stood his ground, but held out the palm of his hand,

encouraging Martin to hand over the knife. The boy was breathing deeply now, working himself up towards even greater fury; night air whistled between the malevolent rictus of his teeth. 'How about it, Martin?'

'f—— your car! And f—— you! You don't want me; you want Deborah. I might even let you have her. But first she's going to have a little present from me. A nice new necklace – a *red* necklace – '

'No!'

The torch crashed to the ground as Deborah cannoned into Montgomery. For some seconds all was confusion, but the fading pound of Martin's footsteps on the path was clear enough.

'I've got her, sir.' Thank God for William Bird.

Montgomery scrabbled against the compact earth and found the lifeless torch.

'Is she all right?' he asked.

'I think so.'

He tapped the torch hard against his hand, and to his relief a thin yellow beam cut a swath through the darkness. Immediately he turned to Deborah.

She cowered like a rabbit who had had a near miss from an articulated lorry. Her cheeks were ashen, the straining eyes were vacant with shock, and shudders convulsed her entire body. But the neck was safe; the thin claret trickle curling lazily down towards her collar-bone had seeped from a superficial one-inch cut.

'Look after Deborah,' he instructed Sergeant Bird. 'Take her back to the car as soon as you can, and radio for some help. I'm going after Martin.'

Without waiting for a reply he started out up the path in an agile sprint, running as fast as he dared while the jolting light picked out hazards strewn ahead. For seventy yards the path was solid, then abruptly it petered out, just as Sergeant Bird had remembered. He paused, controlling his own respirations while he listened for those of Martin. The boy was either climbing the bank above or he had crossed the railway lines. The only other alternative was the tunnel.

Montgomery swept the area above him with the torch-beam:

nothing. He tried to probe the tunnel mouth but it was too far away; the faint yellow finger of light was crushed by the dark press of night. Across the tracks nothing moved; Montgomery skirted the weeds and stepped out on to the wooden sleepers: they offered better progress than the uneven ground alongside. This small branch line was not electrified. He set off again in a loping jog, and soon the brick-rimmed Stygian cavern materialized ahead.

He stopped. As if in answer to an unspoken question, there was an echoing clatter inside – Martin!

Montgomery turned once, scanning the silent valley behind him, then followed his quarry into the tunnel.

Sergeant Bird and Deborah were having a difficult time in the dark. She had started to ask him questions, he wanted to concentrate on finding the quickest way to the car in order to rush help to Montgomery. Fears pulled at his gut with importunate hands: visions of missing the vital path through the allotments; chilling images of Montgomery lying stabbed through the heart.

Suddenly he became aware of a vague humming sound, a low burr from the track ahead. Even before dim lights winked in the distance, he had identified the noise and whirled round towards the tunnel, cupping his hands into a makeshift megaphone.

'Train!' he yelled. 'Train coming!'

He had no idea where Montgomery was, but his scalp crawled with premonitory horror. He watched as a laden goods train juddered its way towards him, resembling a long dark beetle in the cutting. The screech of metal on metal became loud, then almost intolerable as it clanked beneath the path where he stood – then it was past, the sound fading, the beetle scurrying to its hole in the ground.

20

Montgomery was well round the curve of the tunnel when he felt the first vibrations beneath his feet.

He knew that Martin could not be far ahead, even though brief sweeps with the torch-beam had failed to pick him out; the boy was probably lurking in one of those wall recesses built for the safety of railway workers. For this reason Montgomery had been proceeding cautiously along the middle of the right-hand track, flashing the light into each shallow chamber he passed. Martin's capacity for ambush was not to be underestimated.

And now a train was coming.

It was distant as yet, but Montgomery was taking no chances. He would press himself into a niche until it passed, then continue the hunt...

A skittering noise resounded to his left. He swung round in a reflex movement, but barely a second later snapped off the torch-beam and hurled himself to the right as something sang through his hair and buried itself with a dull *clunk* at the base of the opposite tunnel wall.

The oldest trick in the book, he thought. The second missile had sounded like a stone; the first was almost certainly a handful of pebbles. That meant Martin still had his knife.

He backed away in the stifling blackness, suddenly unsure of his direction. The tremor in the ground was now more marked, and he could hear a rhythmic thrumming somewhere behind him. If he used the torch to check his position, Martin might come leaping from his place of concealment...

Montgomery's ankle struck the metal rail, and he gave a

short grunt of pain. The next moment a body slammed into him, knocking him down, jarring his spine against the same rail as twelve stone of cursing fury grappled to grind him into the earth. The torch shot from his hand, lost for good this time, and he felt hot breath spurt against his face.

Martin clawed at him with the strength of the demented; Montgomery, hyperextended in the shape of a bow, could do little to defend himself. The hard rail beneath him was now juddering fiercely, and he could hear individual squeaks above the pulsating chug of the train. Yet even in the confusion and gathering noise, he realized that neither of Martin's hands held the knife. To use it, he needed a few seconds' grace, and this Montgomery was determined to deny him.

A sinister light flickered against the soot-caked wall opposite, and then became fixed. The din of the train echoed through the tunnel, painful in its intensity. As Montgomery clung on grimly to Martin's muscular wrists the locomotive itself appeared, lumbering but powerful, like some prehistoric monster. Martin gave no sign of noticing; his mind was too far gone in hatred.

Desperately, Montgomery thrashed as a heavy weight descended on his windpipe. What a stupid way to die ... He heard the scream of metal as brakes were applied and the wheels locked, but still the machine rushed onwards. In the last deafening seconds before impact he focused all his strength into his arms, burst free of the stranglehold and flung himself into the gravel between the two tracks, pulling Martin with him.

The train thundered past inches from his back; Martin had lost his positional advantage, but still he struggled and strained. Montgomery had no hesitation. The Queensberry rules had long been ignored by his adversary; now it was his turn.

Moments later, Martin lay gasping, all his fight gone.

Frobisher rang Montgomery the next day.

'Thought you might like to hear the news from the lab,' he

said. 'They've found the drug propranolol in samples taken from George Witherspoon's body.'

'Ah.' Montgomery had no knowledge of the properties of this drug, but felt he could make a shrewd guess. 'Tell me about it,' he invited.

'It's one of a group of compounds known as beta-blockers, which are used to treat a variety of medical conditions, in particular high blood pressure, angina and cardiac arrhythmias. But asthmatics should avoid them like the plague, even the so-called "cardioselective" brands. Beta-blockers precipitate bronchospasm.'

'You mean they actually trigger asthma attacks?'

'That's right. They're very dangerous for ányone with respiratory insufficiency.'

'You mentioned angina just now. Might someone who had already experienced a heart attack be taking propranolol as their medication?'

'Yes, indeed. They can make a second attack less likely.'

Mr Lampkin . . . Montgomery's suspicions were being vindicated, but one puzzle remained: how had Martin acquired his knowledge, considering his lack of formal education? Perhaps, in just one area, he had told the truth . . .

'I don't understand,' Jackson said later. 'Where did Martin get the tablets, if he never visited his father's surgery?'

Montgomery sat down at Sergeant Bird's desk as the team of detectives looked to him for answers. 'He used the Lampkins,' he said, 'people who trusted him and thought the world of him. If you'll permit me to start at the beginning, I'll explain the story as far as we've been able to unravel it.

'We know that Martin has always been aware that he was unwanted by Lynn. Children have a sharp instinct for such things, and even though she spoiled him in compensation, he saw through this to the truth. When Deborah came along, the contrast in Lynn's attitude was clear. This was *her* baby, not one foisted upon her. From that point, Martin behaved so

181

badly that strict parental discipline for Deborah became inevitable. The more uncontrollable he became, the more she was subject to rules and regulations which he rightly interpreted as some of the harsher signs of love. He longed for similar tokens for himself, but his own behaviour ensured that this rarely happened. By the time Martin had stolen a car at the age of fifteen, his largest overt act of rebellion, Neville had given up trying completely.

'Martin lived a semi-detached life from that point, using Oaklands as a hotel rather than a home, spending his time with rough individuals and dressing accordingly. He also developed a taste for gambling: first the fruit machines, later the casino. His semi-skilled job couldn't provide funds to sustain this kind of activity, so he began housebreaking.'

Montgomery looked up. 'I discovered something interesting about Martin's little weekend essays into philanthropy. The two couples he worked for prior to the Lampkins were both robbed early on a Sunday morning by a burglar entering through an unlocked rear window. They were elderly people, confused, and neither could remember releasing the window themselves, but they were uniform in their insistence that the nice boy who came to do the garden couldn't possibly have been involved.

'The Lampkins would have been next. He went to their bungalow on Saturdays to prepare the ground – in more ways than one – but while he was there, Hilda Lampkin gave him an idea. Like most elderly ladies, she loved discussing her ailments with anyone who would listen, and she told Martin about the thrombosis in her leg. She was on that warfarin to thin the blood, and had to go for regular tests at the hospital, and the doctors said she must avoid alcohol and aspirins and be sure not to take too many tablets or she might bleed to death ... Martin stole some forthwith, because he had just heard the first rumblings about Maud and the will.'

'Wait,' said Jackson. 'That doesn't make sense. Why did Martin risk poisoning his grandmother with a long-acting drug like warfarin if he didn't want to be disinherited? She lived to change the will; if the altered document had proved valid, he'd have lost the lot.'

182

'We were looking at it from the wrong perspective,' answered Montgomery. 'It was actually much simpler than we imagined. We thought Martin had no motive for killing Maud because she died *after* changing her will. In addition, his last visit to her room had been on the Wednesday, a full forty-eight hours before her haemorrhage. We didn't know at that stage how warfarin works ... *neither did Martin*. He expected an "instant poison" when he doctored her fruit crumble, and must have felt very thwarted to find that it didn't act in time. When he came to make his bogus confession, he cleverly fed us the idea that Maud had shared with him the joke about the will – so even if we did determine when the drug had been given, he would still have had no apparent motive.

'Martin felt that the family owed him ... once the idea of inheritance income was in his head, it was a short step from murdering Maud to disposing of George as well. The circumstances of Maud's death had led to her being buried without suspicion; if Martin was careful, and engineered something natural-looking for George, he would avoid attracting undue attention. Like Maud, George was an invalid; it should be possible to come up with an idea.

'Here, I think, is the only area where Martin told us the truth. He said his medical knowledge had come from Neville's books. We were sceptical because it was widely known that Martin had never shown the remotest interest in the subject, and we also knew his educational deficiencies. But education and intelligence don't always go hand in hand: Martin has plenty of the latter. He wasn't interested in books telling you how to cure people. He wanted to know what happens when medicine goes wrong.

'In common with all doctors, Neville is obliged to subscribe to a defence society, in his case the Hippocratic Guardians. He receives an annual report, and keeps the copies in his study. These booklets outline all kinds of horror stories where mistakes have occurred in hospital or general practice and the victims or their relatives have seen fit to sue. They're published primarily as object lessons to others.

'One recent case described a hospital error where a beta-blocking drug was given to an asthmatic instead of a compound for long-term prophylaxis. The trade names of the two are very similar, and the doctor had scrawled his prescription on the treatment card in handwriting instead of capitals. This patient died . . .

'I'm convinced that Martin read this, and saw that Mr Lampkin had a supply of the same drug in his home. Just like the unfortunate patient, George was not only deprived of his normal medication, but given something lethal to people with his kind of breathing problem. Both types of tablet are pink.'

'Then the cat was completely innocent!' exclaimed Smythe.

'That's right. On the Saturday of George's death, Martin returned from his digging three-quarters of an hour before his parents. He saw the body slumped in the chair as he had expected, and Henry in the conservatory, recovering from his ordeal in Mr Balfour's sycamore. Now, Henry detests Martin, but can't resist catmint. My theory is that Martin dragged a bunch of the herb along the floor, enticing Henry to follow, then trailed it over George's lap. We know from Angela Cording that this was a game Martin played as a child. Once Henry was on George's knees Martin flicked away the bait and let Henry catch the scent of the sprigs he had inserted into the trouser pockets. The cat was happy to curl up and make himself comfortable.'

'That accounts for the lack of a struggle,' said Sergeant Bird.

'Yes. Poor George was long gone; Martin simply relocked all the doors and took himself off again until he knew someone else would have made the discovery.'

'So he hoped to get away with it,' said Jackson.

'Very much so. There's nothing visible at autopsy which will distinguish drug-induced bronchospasm from other forms of bronchial asthma. George's death would have gone down in the records as due to a natural cause, and that would have been that. Martin couldn't have anticipated either Harriet Lawson's persistent interference or Deborah's flight, although he kept his wits about him regarding Deborah. When he saw her note on the dressing-table, he took it, just in case it should prove useful. If she quickly returned, he could always pretend it had fluttered under the bed.

184

'Things became serious for Martin when our lab analysis revealed that warfarin had killed Maud. The opportunity to administer poison was obviously greatest among members of the Oaklands household, and as outside investigators, police would tend to concentrate on crude motives like money. Martin's best strategy was to try to misdirect us, to acquaint us with the human tensions which had existed in the family. He did this most successfully.'

Montgomery maintained his pale poker face, but inside he felt another flare of shame. The meaning of 'Is he good?' was now perfectly clear. Martin might just as well have asked: 'Will he keep me in clink while he checks out my alibi? I do hope so.' Sloppy police work might have left gaps, laid him open to suspicions of priming Ray; instead, they had been diligent and played straight into his hands. Martin had confessed to both crimes because his alibi for the second was strong.

'Presumably it was at this point that he decided to implicate Deborah,' mused William Bird. 'Her absence was most convenient for him. For instance, I remember he told us about the drug samples at his father's surgery. Deborah must have described the cupboard to him after her visit.'

'Yes. If the blame could be shifted to Deborah, not only would he be in the clear, but he would be a hundred per cent better off financially. Potent motives, when you consider how much he always hated her.'

'Where did she go?' asked Jackson. 'Why were we unable to trace her route from Thorbeck?'

'Ah; Deborah fooled us by scrupulously avoiding the village telephone box. Instead, she staggered back to Aileen's house with her suitcase and cat basket while Mrs Blanchard was still absent, recruited Aileen to the cause and left Henry in the garden shed overnight. Deborah herself, suitably made up, took a bus from the Clarkwood Estate into the centre of town, where she consulted the Yellow Pages and arranged to stay two nights at the Awsworth bed-and-breakfast place; it was all she could afford. On Sunday morning she returned for Henry, and took him to Miss Goodridge's animal sanctuary for safe-keeping. She used a careful combination of buses, taxis and

Aileen's bicycle for her travels. From Monday night onwards, with no further resources, she lived in the Blanchards' shed herself – one very determined young woman.'

He gave a rueful smile. 'Are there any more questions?'

The detectives shook their heads, some staring at the ground, and it was a few seconds before Smythe's soft voice edged its way into the silence.

'Did Martin kill Beverley Taylor, sir, or did she do it herself?'

'He as good as murdered her. Beverley was a nuisance, pestering him about the child. He saw a way in which her vulnerability could be put to use, promising her pills if she would make a telephone call for him. We know from Josie how reluctant she was; the distress PC Jenkins heard was quite genuine. Martin must have coached her to speak with Deborah's enunciation. He may even have been present when she made the call.

'Perhaps he hoped the warfarin alone would prove lethal. Or maybe he told her that if nothing happened after so many hours she was to try more direct means. But without the warfarin, she might not have bled to death.'

This time the silence lasted longer.

21

'Well, do you like the view?'

Katherine Adams smiled at Montgomery as he stood by the open french windows of her dining-room. Outside, a narrow stone terrace constituted the only level ground; beyond this the terrain plunged steeply, a half-wild garden of shrubs and mature trees, in places almost a scree, until it reached the bottom a hundred feet below. Here stood most of the gracious Victorian buildings in the area known as 'the Park': once the domiciles of wealthy industrialists, many were now subdivided into students' flats.

'It's spectacular,' he said. Only the dizzying vista from the castle parapet could compete in his experience, and that gave too much precedence to the dingier aspects of Nottingham. In the Park, the impression of bygone elegance and good taste was enduring.

'There's a similar outlook from the back of the Victoria Hospital,' she told him. 'I enjoyed my time there, despite the personal troubles at home, so when Herman had gone and this house came up for sale, I threw everything into the kitty to buy it. To have this view, and yet live within walking distance of the town centre – that's a rare privilege.'

A snatch of breeze made the curtain next to Montgomery billow. He took a sip of the Pimm's she had given him and feasted his eyes for the last time.

'My dinner guests all vie for the end chairs,' she went on. 'On summer evenings we keep the french doors open for an *al fresco* ambience.'

We ... such an important word. It meant companionship,

moral support, common purpose – yet Montgomery had ascertained that Katherine Adams lived alone. That struck him as somehow tragic.

He put down the glass. 'Thank you for the drink,' he said.

'Thank you for coming to tell me I'm no longer under suspicion. I always imagined the police were too busy to give feedback to their witnesses.'

'That's usually the case.' Montgomery refrained from mendaciously claiming he had just been passing anyway; that would insult her intelligence. He followed her into the hall, pausing again at the hedgerow painting. In a moment, he would be out in the street, yet an unforgivably personal question was beating in his brain, demanding that he give it voice. With his arm he made a sweeping gesture which embraced the whole house.

'Is this enough?' he asked.

She didn't need to ask what he meant.

'It is for me,' she said. 'I relish being mistress of my own destiny, not an apologist for someone else's frailties. The decisions I make can stand or fall on their own merits without outside interference. The new practice, for instance. Another Herman would never stand for it.'

'What's this?'

'Oh, I'm leaving Venning Road soon. A former colleague of mine, Dr Blake, is setting up a new practice in Wollaton and has asked me to join him as an equal partner. It'll mean more night work, but my daytime surgeries won't be full of malcontents from Neville's and Kenneth's lists. I haven't been happy at Venning Road for some time, and when Bernard leaves I expect the new regime will be even more restrictive. The choice was between moaning and doing something about it.'

Montgomery thought he detected a humorous glint in her eye as she continued: 'Barbara Tarrant is coming to join us, and I shall have at least one patient. Judge Atherton has kindly asked if he and his wife can be registered with me at the new premises; they're a lovely couple and I shall be delighted to attend them. So in answer to your question, Inspector Montgomery, any apparently fallow areas in my life will be balanced by this greater challenge at work. The basic selfishness of living alone will not only complement the work but be a necessity. There will be no truly empty moments.'

She smiled once more as she opened the door for him, and Montgomery wondered whether the notion of waste he still felt was simply due to masculine incomprehension. He had sensed fire beyond her cool beauty, like that of a smouldering opal. In other circumstances he might have stretched out his hand towards the flame, could he have done so with honour. One day, he hoped somebody would, someone free who would respect her situation, and perhaps by then Katherine Adams would be ready to trust again.

He left.

'It was kind of you to call and tell me about Deborah,' said Angela Cording. 'Lynn did ring yesterday, although she didn't say much.'

'We've been very grateful for your help,' countered Montgomery. He looked round at the paper-strewn room, where Minou in the corner gnawed at an unwound spool of typewriter-correction tape. 'I can see that you're busy, but there's just one thing that I'd like to ask you.'

'Fire away!'

'Martin . . . ' Her face grew grim. 'He has a scar above his left eyebrow. Do you know how he came by it?'

'Ye-es. It was a fracas with Deborah.'

'What exactly happened?'

'He was torturing Henry, and . . .'

Of course.

'Martin used to steal from my purse,' said Lynn Witherspoon. 'The first two occasions, I told Neville, but he refused to believe it. He insisted I was imagining things, that I'd been careless with the money. Eventually the pilfering stopped; Martin must have decided it was more fruitful to look elsewhere, as you discovered. Anyway, please accept my thanks for everything you've done, especially for Deborah.'

Montgomery inclined his head, feeling surprise at the degree of openness she displayed in the absence of Neville. 'I'm glad Deborah's recovered well from the shock,' he said.

Their eyes moved with one accord to the window; outside in the garden they could see Deborah crouched by the border, working at the soil with a hand-fork. By her side was the substantial form of Henry.

'Child-woman,' said Lynn softly. 'She and Aileen both. Do you know something, Inspector? For a while I actually thought that Deborah might have done these awful things. It was the only possible explanation . . . I thought she'd done them to save my sanity. Isn't that terrible! I could never confide in Neville, but now that we know the truth I feel I have to tell someone.

'Deborah was reluctant to go in to Maud on the day she died. I was in a flap – for the first time I'd left Maud alone and gone to the cinema in town. They were showing a film about Eleanor of Aquitaine, which was of no interest to Neville. Maud usually dozed in the afternoons. Unfortunately, I missed my bus and had to catch the same one Deborah was on. I got off at the previous stop and positively *sprinted* to the green! Deborah was usually very good about seeing to her grandmother, but on this particular afternoon she demurred. I remembered that later . . . along with other things, it made me wonder.'

Montgomery knew Deborah had found the body: that had been one reason he had felt ambivalent about Lynn herself as a murder suspect. What mother would let the daughter she loved make such a gruesome discovery? And could she then stand by and let that daughter herself shoulder the blame by dint of running away? Maybe some people could, but not this woman.

They glanced towards the window again as Deborah finished her weeding and strode off towards the compost heap with a laden box, Henry in close pursuit.

'Yes, Deborah's growing up,' went on Lynn. 'Neville's beginning to accept it now. He's even coming to terms with the fact that she'll never be an academic. He's listening to what she *really* wants, which is a career in catering. She's very good with her hands.'

'Not a veterinary assistant?' asked Montgomery.

'No; she says she couldn't bear to see an animal put down.'

They didn't mention Martin, but once again he hung in both their minds. Martin had been gifted with intelligence; if he had channelled it properly he might have forged a career to be proud of, and gained the bonus of Neville's esteem. Instead all was squandered. His sentence would give him a decade to dwell on that.

'What do you *mean*, Judge Atherton is transferring to Katherine Adams's list? Didn't you have a word with Bernard? Didn't he even *try* to use his influence?' Trudi Forester lowered her magazine and stared incredulously at Kenneth.

'Trudi, this is entirely a matter for the judge himself.'

'Well, I think it smacks of poaching. I must say I'm astonished at Katherine's behaviour. It's so inconsiderate, leaving just when the practice most needs her.'

'We'll get by; she's promised to stay on until Bernard's replacement is established.'

'How thoughtful! What about all the community duties she was supposed to be covering, not to mention the famous Menopause Clinic? The trainees won't be able to take those on straight away.'

'Er . . . no.'

Trudi stood up, and plucked a small piece of fluff from her sleeve with impatient fingers. 'It beats me how you allowed this to happen,' she snapped. 'Still, I suppose there'll be time for you to work out how best to manage this new state of affairs. Now we must get ready for the Lord Mayor's Reception.'

'What?'

'I told you Prunella Petherbridge was buying tickets for us.'

'Drat; I thought that was next week. I'm sorry, Trudi, but I can't come. I've got to check over my First Aid notes, and give a lecture to the Red Cross. Katherine had another commitment, and Neville asked me ... ' He broke off as Trudi's nostrils flared with rage. She paced the room, obviously controlling herself with some effort, then turned on him.'God, Kenneth,' she said bitterly. 'You're such a weed.'

'Welcome!' William Bird ushered Montgomery and Carole through the doorway of his home into the comfortable interior. Both were familiar with his large, book-lined sitting-room, having been invited sporadically over the years for drinks, but the offer of a meal was a rare treat; Sergeant Bird was extremely reticent about his culinary prowess in relation to Carole's. Tonight, however, a delicious meaty aroma emanated from the kitchen.

'I'm doing beef and ale casserole,' he announced.

He took their coats, and they moved towards the fireplace where the high-backed chairs stood. Carole reached the one he usually offered her, his own favourite, and found herself staring down at a black and white cat. Sam's eyes were closed, but he stretched sinuously as if aware of their presence, covering even more of the seat's surface area.

'Er, I hope you don't mind having this chair tonight,' said William Bird hesitantly, pulling out the adjacent one. 'I don't like to disturb Sam when he's settled.'

Montgomery began to grin. 'Just who *is* the boss round here?' he asked. 'You or the cat?'

Sam snored.

192